MW01482316

Fireweed Island

By
Mary E. Dickson

To Maritta,
Comrades-in-arms,
Love
Mary

Strategic Book Publishing and Rights Co.

Copyright © 2013.
All rights reserved by Mary E. Dickson.

Book Design/Layout by Kalpart. Visit www.kalpart.com

No part of this book may be reproduced or transmitted in any form
or by any means, graphic, electronic, or mechanical including
photocopying, recording, taping or by any information retrieval
system, without the permission in writing of the publisher.

Strategic Book Publishing and Rights Co.
12620 FM 1960, Suite A4-507
Houston TX 77065
www.sbpra.com

ISBN: 978-1-62516-206-9

For my parents:

Gordon Clive Dickson
and
Mildred Florence Dickson.

Acknowledgments

I am deeply grateful to my friend Gayle Lynn Kerr for reading each chapter, for her comments, encouragement and her unwavering belief in me when I lost belief in myself, and Cynthia Whitson, for her wicked wit and humor that pulled me through the dark.

AUSTRALIA, 2005

I heard the distinctive low growl of our silver Mercedes while slipping as smoothly as a silent shark into our carport. It was my husband, Tom, returning from work. Retired, he had a small job working for an airport service transporting passengers to and from the airport. I glanced at the kitchen clock. Six p.m. He's late. This meant trouble. I quickly turned the gas up to medium high under the simmering pasta pot. Tom would be famished. Behind me, I heard the screen door forcefully slide open and then violently pushed back with a loud snap. I remained standing with my back to him, watching the pasta sauce bubble softly, making small popping sounds. I could not turn and raise my eyes to his face. His anger was palpable and a clear threat. I heard his briefcase crash to the wooden floor with a loud bang. Now his jacket was tossed, and it slithered a small ways down the hall, buttons scraping the wooden floor. His duffel bag fell with a thump. Lastly, I heard him roughly kick his shoes off without unlacing them, leaving them for me to pick up and put away. Only then did I lift my eyes to his face.

"Tom?"

He turned his back to me without a word then stomped down the hall to his den. My eyes followed his lean, stooped back as he entered the room, shutting the door firmly behind him, shutting me out as well. He was seventy years of age. I was sixty. I wanted peace in my life now. This behavior was not an isolated event, this contempt for me, this sudden locking me out. We had only been married for two short years. His attitude had changed radically since we became married. As soon as the ink was dry on our marriage certificate, he changed from charming to autocratic. A nagging question that I had been choosing to ignore and pushing away scratched to the surface of my mind once again and begged to be looked at: Had I made a drastic mistake in marrying Tom?

I returned to the stove and stared transfixed into the depths of the swift, rumbling water in the pasta pot. I carefully slid in the spaghetti strands in small bunches. The steam from the pot curled around me. Only the soft tick of our kitchen clock disturbed the thick silence. I breathed in the pungent spicy aroma of the warmed spaghetti sauce. A pang of disappointment about my present circumstances and my inability to change my situation lay shallow in my gut and lodged there. I was sixty years old and still as unsettled as I had been during my teenage years.

With the pasta cooked and the sauce warmed through, I drained the spaghetti then called out, "Tom, dinner!"

No response. I walked down to the den and knocked softly, opened the door quietly, then poked my head through the doorway.

"Didn't you hear me, Tom?"

He quickly picked up a newspaper from his desk, ignoring me. I observed him turn the pages over obsessively, giving the print a quick cursory glance. His eyes darted over the pages, feigning interest. When I didn't leave, he began to shake and snap the pages violently to straighten them. My heart sank. He was going to be unreasonable once again.

My eyes quickly scanned the room. The light of the late afternoon sun was blocked by dusty brown velvet curtains that he never allowed to be opened. The air was dense, stale with cigarette smoke. His ashtray was overflowing. Every surface was grimy and thick with dust. Tom did not allow me in here without his presence. I noticed something new; he had placed a lock on his file cabinet.

I reigned in my impatience and repeated evenly, "Tom, dinner!"

His razor sharp words sliced right through me.

"It's ready?"

Wariness crept into my senses. I recognized the timbre in his voice. Without a doubt, something had upset Tom today. I was far too aware of what that portended. I watched him for a moment, holding my breath, and waited for him to make a move.

His next words were brusque and irritated.

"Hold off. I am reading something."

The abrupt ring of the telephone startled us both. Tom appeared very nervous. This alarmed me. *What's going on?* He hastily picked up the receiver, and then he impatiently cocked his head toward the door, motioning me to leave.

When I hesitated, he hissed, "Go now, and shut the door behind you!"

I silently returned to the stove to lower the heat, yet again. The pasta would be limp, the sauce overcooked. I would be blamed for that, too. I overheard Tom's voice. It sounded like a heated discussion, if I could go by Tom's urgent, angry tone. His voice was muffled, so I could not make out his words. My anxiety sped up several knots. Since we got married, he had transformed from a congenial person into a mean, spiteful bully.

It was over half an hour before Tom finally slunk out from the den. He stomped loudly over to the dining table and plopped down in his chair without a word. He sat stiffly erect, hands on his lap, waiting impatiently for me to serve him. A brooding silence enclosed around us like acid smog, asphyxiating any hope I had of a congenial meal.

Tom's behavior stirred in me a memory of lonely, silent meals and frightening emptiness that dominated my life with my mother after my father died. I inhaled deeply, then let out a huge sigh before I brought his plate to the table and placed it in front of him. This feeling of servitude that he instilled in me was diminishing my spirit.

I went back to the stove, brought my own plate to the table and then sat down across from him. I still hoped to begin a pleasant conversation between us.

I said as lightly as I could manage, "How was your day, Tom? Traffic heavy?"

His reply dripped with sarcasm. "Maddy, how was your *day*? Did you find a job?"

I hampered down my anger. I compelled my words to be measured and even as I sat across the table.

"It's not for lack of trying. I am not a permanent resident of Australia, after all."

He turned to face me. His expression was nasty.

"There is nothing, do you hear me, nothing I can't employ someone else to do here! All you do around here are menial tasks!"

Though the threat in Tom's voice was both real and frightening, and I knew better, I responded in anger, regardless of the consequences.

"What do you mean, menial tasks—cooking, cleaning, laundry, gardening—all that?"

Tom looked me up and down with icy condescension. The tension built up around us like threatening thunder clouds looming on the horizon.

I shot a sidewise glance at Tom across the table. I fought to remain calm. I responded to his wrath earlier, and it was a bad mistake in judgment. I tried to appear nonchalant. I casually reached for a bun from the basket in front of me to distract him. I glimpsed out of the corner of my eye at him. He ate so methodically, so exactly, now a forkful of spaghetti, now a bite of bread, now a slurp of water, and again a forkful of spaghetti, repeating the sequence again and again. He held his baby finger aloft from the rest. His affectations and pretentiousness repulsed me now.

Recently, he ceased caring about his appearance. His hair was greasy and in need of a wash. A fine dust of dandruff lay on the shoulders of his navy blue uniform. The stark contrast between his slovenly appearance and his precise mannerisms astounded me. He also had stopped trying to please me. What changed, and why so quickly?

I staggered under the weight of a new hypothesis about my situation. I saw before me a conundrum of small events that would set a stream of panic in me if I had the guts to unravel them and face them squarely. How long could I hold the reality of my situation at bay?

A part of me had already intuited—no, knew—that he was still in love with Paula. Paula and Tom had known each other for over thirty years. Was he seeing her again? I realized, too late, that for Tom the relationship with Paula was the hunt that never ended, the prey he could never capture. Paula's last refusal to marry him was Tom's last straw. He married me in revenge. He now realized he married me for nothing. Paula didn't care, and that was Tom's Waterloo.

Betrayal and resentment burned like acid in my stomach. Tom said that things were over between him and Paula, that I was paranoid. But *were* they finished? Tom clearly liked the chase. The minute I married him my confidence shattered. That was because the second we began to live together, his desire for me disappeared. Now that he recognized that he would not receive the desired response about our marriage from Paula, he saw me as a heavy, unwanted burden.

I remained silent. I swallowed down the burning rage that worked up my throat. Fear of the consequences halted me from responding to his stupid accusations. I was terrified that I would say something to further escalate his hostility.

Waiting for what was to come, I continued to watch with revulsion as Tom pushed his spaghetti around on his plate with his fork. Without warning, he pulled a thin strand of spaghetti away from the rest. He picked it off his fork with his flaccid fingers, his pinky up, and then he swung it to and fro in front of my nose.

This was too much to ignore. I could not overlook this stupidity.

"What are you doing?"

"Did you boil the water before you put the spaghetti in?" he snarled, challenging a reply.

I was momentarily immobilized by my loathing and disgust for this monster in front of me. Next, as unexpectedly as a lightning bolt, apprehension shot through me. My mind took over. As quickly as the inertia came over me, it retreated. I became fully alert. I was fully back in the present moment. My senses became vigilant, my mind cautious and watchful. I knew that any sign of weakness would show my vulnerability. That would cost me dearly, perhaps even my life. I picked up my own fork and pulled up some spaghetti strands from my plate.

It took effort to say lightly, "Of course, I did."

Tom took the limp strand of spaghetti, leaned over close to me and then flung it to and fro in front of my eyes.

"What's this then, eh?"

I examined my plate for any stiff spaghetti strands and found none.

"My spaghetti is okay."

I was careful to avert my eyes from Tom. I couldn't allow Tom any further excuse to escalate his antagonism toward me. It was too dangerous. The whole progression of events was surreal. I was living in a vortex, and I was being sucked into its very centre.

In an odd second of occurrence, I noticed Tom pick up his plate, watched as it flew towards me in slow motion. I stood up quickly, but the tablecloth tangled up in front of me and got caught in my belt. I tried frantically to unravel the cloth and move away. After several attempts, I finally broke free, but too late. Tom's dinner plate of spaghetti struck me in the gut, thumping the breath out of me. I struggled to catch my breath. Red, hot, sticky sauce streamed down my stomach and torso like hot volcanic lava, searing my skin. A knife-sharp pain cut right through me. I stood still in cold shock, unable to move. When I finally managed to catch my breath, raw emotion erupted inside me and boiled over.

I screamed, "You are a crazy bastard!"

Tom's sharp eyes stabbed right through me. Instantly, my blood turned to ice. With trembling hands, I quickly drew my clothes away from my scorched body. I raced to the bathroom and shut the door. Hastily, I peeled off my clothes. I tossed them into the laundry tub to soak and turned the cold water tap on until it was full. I was sticky. I was afraid to shower and be caught there. I decided to sponge myself off. I was terrified that the violence in Tom had not abated. My heart still leapt erratically up and down like Mexican jumping beans.

Everything I loathed about Tom and everything I loathed about myself gripped me with such force that I slipped down to the floor and sat on the cold hard tiles, my head on my knees. I needed fresh clothes from the bedroom. With only my towel wrapped around me, I couldn't chance putting myself within distance of Tom's long, strong arms. I reached for my gardening clothes in the laundry basket where I had tossed them earlier that afternoon. They were damp, reeked of perspiration and were badly wrinkled, but I rapidly put them on anyway. Cautiously, I reentered the kitchen where Tom was still seated at the table. The red, messy goo remained on the carpet. I felt Tom's eyes watch my every move as I bent down painfully to pick up the shards of broken plate amongst the spaghetti sauce. Dark stains were splattered on the rug, like bloodshed after a shooting.

It looks like something out of CSI, I thought. Then, *I won't be able to remove the stain.* Immediately it occurred to me that it didn't matter anymore. Nothing did. My whole life was permanently stained by this sadistic man.

While I was bent down a razor sharp sting pierced my upper and lower back. A heavy silver fork, a dinner knife, rebounded off my back. The shrill clatter of silverware fell to the floor, penetrating the silence of the room. Another jolt of pain struck me as I slumped to the floor in agony. With all the effort that I could summon, I pulled up a weak tangled breath from the depth of my sore abdomen, one after another until I could breathe normally. Only then did I slowly drag myself upright.

Tom grunted something unintelligible as he headed back into his den, closing the door sharply behind him.

I knew from experience that he would hole himself up there until he was ready for bed. Once his anger had been spent, he relaxed without another thought about what he had done. I returned to the bathroom where I found ointment in the medicine cabinet. I soaked a pad of cotton wool and applied it as well as I could to the stinging wounds on my back.

I returned to the kitchen to clean up. Good habits were hard to break. When I was finished, I made myself an instant coffee in my blue mug and took it to the living room. The small living room was cold, dark, and musty. I longed for my spacious, serene condo I had left in Canada.

I pushed Tom's old newspapers aside on the coffee table

and set my coffee down to cool. I slouched down into an old, uncomfortable chair Tom had found along the side of a road on trash day. It stunk of old perspiration. No matter how much I tried, I could not dispel the sickening stench. It was upholstered in an old green felt, shiny in numerous places, rubbed down to a thin skein where an elbow, ass, or back had rubbed against it for years. Any length of time spent in the chair was pure torture. Springs had sprung apart and poked through the material. They jabbed me in my back and butt. I shifted around in the chair to avoid them, but it was impossible.

I began to assess my situation. Tom counted on what I just acknowledged to myself. I couldn't leave him without money, without hope of a job, without assistance from the Australian government because I was not a permanent resident of Australia. I was now without family or friends' support. Tom took full advantage of the isolation he forced upon me and my lack of income. I was stuck like a fly on a flypaper cone.

My thoughts reeled back to the mysterious phone call Tom had received earlier this evening. Had it been Paula?

I recognized at that moment the full impact of the fact that my marriage effectively ended not long after our marriage ceremony. I had to face the devastating realization that he married me to seek revenge on Paula, who, over a span of thirty years, had continually refused to marry him. The situation was pathetic, really. I was no more than a kept woman. Tom and I didn't come close to being in any kind of partnership. My hope of a loving relationship fizzled out like a faulty firework that sizzled, then collapsed and expired before it could take off to burst into flames.

Sitting in this chair was sheer torture, so I slipped to the floor. I leaned my back against it and closed my eyes. I let the past surface. I was no longer in Australia but back in my old childhood home, sitting at the oak dining table on a summer morning, waiting for our housekeeper, Anna, to bring me my porridge and toast. Memories floated up of our Pekinese dog, Tina, sitting at my bare feet, warming them, and the sound of father coming in the side door from his early morning walk in the field, bringing the scent of the fresh air mingled with the whiff of tobacco with him.

All the hurts and grievances from the past sprung alive in me as old painful memories emerged. The first memory took place one summer day in 1955. I was twelve years old. My sister was fifteen.

FIREWEED ISLAND, 1955

The summer I was five, catastrophe struck our small family. We had to leave the mining village of Bralorne because Father contracted silicosis and could no longer work. We moved to one of my grandfather's large houses on Fireweed Island. It was a bitter disappointment for my mother, losing father's income and having to accept her father's charity.

The year-rounders had the sleepy island all to themselves until the summer. There were only a few families living scattered on the small, peaceful island. We all kept more or less to ourselves. Once, I overheard a neighbor say that our mother thought she was a cut above the rest of the residents on the island. I would guess that would be true, because I often heard her say to one of her sisters about her sister-in-law, "She's not one of our kind." My sister, Erin, and I, along with my cousins, loved the excitement that summer brought. Mother felt the invasion of the tourists and the loss of our serenity during the summer months more than anybody.

The summer I was twelve was the hottest on record. The huge maple trees that grew between my grandmother's house and ours provided a mammoth umbrella, shading us from the hot sun. I took my library books and my writing notebook and lay on a quilt under them for most of the day. Father's garden bloomed with roses, hydrangea, and lavender. Luckily, we had our own well, so water at our place was not a problem. The interior of our house was stifling. The smothering heat in the city brought tourists to our island in swarms, covering our land like locusts on a wheat field.

My cousins, Connor and Lily, lived next door in Grandma's

house. Lily was ten, two years younger than me, and Connor was thirteen, one year older. At twelve years of age, I was still a tomboy, climbing trees, playing run sheep run with my cousins and the neighbors' kids, making rafts to sail over the lake and swimming. I hung out with my cousins away from the house so I wouldn't have to deal with Mother's temper and erratic mood swings.

Let me tell you something I learned: sometimes people have a parent whose approval they crave their entire lives and never fully receive. Lots of things can happen to a person because of that. I guess I am not the first person who had grown up knowing that my birth was an unhappy occurrence. It was that way with me. I seemed to be a magnet to all of Mother's anger and the recipient of all the toxic waste of Mother's depression.

My story really begins on the first speedboat race of the summer. I was told that the cracker box boats went up to speeds of seventy-five miles an hour on the average of five laps on a five-mile course. Usually, the races brought two thousand fans to our little island. It was a huge event.

I was still getting dressed in my bedroom when I heard Lily's excited voice downstairs.

"Is Maddy up?"

I heard Anna, our cook, reply, "Hush, Lily. Your aunt and uncle are having breakfast. Maddy's not come down yet. I'll send Maddy over to you when she has finished her breakfast."

I was so excited! We could see all the thrills up close then, not just from my small bedroom window or by watching from the branches of the walnut tree next to our garage.

Chock-full of anticipation, I bounded down the stairs to our dining room. The smell of bacon and eggs made my mouth water. I raced into the dining room. Erin, Father, and Mother were silently eating their breakfast. A thick cloud of tension draped over the room. Only the soft clanging of silverware and the muted clink of silver against fine china tea saucers pierced the dense silence.

At first glance, I could clearly see that Mother was highly agitated over the earsplitting noise coming from the boat races. So

I knew from experience to hide my excitement about attending the races.

Mother got up from the table and started to walk in circles. I quietly and very carefully walked past her over to my place at the table. Cautiously, I picked up my chair and pulled it up from the floor and away from the table. I set it down softly. Silently, I slipped in.

My head was as light as a helium balloon; anxiety did that to me. I lost my appetite. Anna, our housemaid, glided over to the side table from the kitchen door and piled my plate high with bacon, eggs, and toast. Soundlessly she brought it over to me, her steps shuffling quietly in her felt slippers. I felt too anxious to eat, but I forced myself to choke down my food. An unclean plate would upset Mother further and make matters worse. The smallest breach of any rule would be met with heavy-handed, cruel mockery, believe me.

I waited for a good moment to speak to Mother. When she finally stopped pacing in circles and sat down at the table again, I seized my opportunity.

I carefully put my spoon down on the bread and butter plate so it wouldn't clink. Although I looked in Mother's direction, I was careful not to look at her directly.

"Mother, may I go watch the races at Swan's Point with Lily and Connor after breakfast? They are leaving at nine o'clock sharp!"

Mother reached for her toast and began to angrily slather it with butter. She slathered butter on her toast over and over until it spilled over and trickled down on her lap. She didn't even look up at me when she replied.

"No, you may not!"

A well of tears threatened to overflow and spill out of my eyes. Arguing would do me no good. I must get myself in order.

Not wanting to incite any further agitation from Mother, Father spoke up gently. "Now, Florence, surely, you promised her last summer."

Mother glared at Father.

"Gordon, don't interfere!"

It was becoming abundantly clear to us all. Mother's irritation was accelerating dangerously, spiraling and spinning out of control.

From the corner of my eye, I noticed Anna approach Mother like greased lightning.

"Anything else, madam?" Clearly, she was trying to divert Mother's attention. I could always count on Anna to protect me, however discreetly.

"Can't you see I am finished, Anna? Clear my plates away."

Anna did as she was told, her mouth in a tight grimace, holding back her temper. Mother rose from the table swiftly, knocking her teacup slightly. The tinkling sound echoed throughout the silent room. We all watched as the teacup teetered then suddenly stopped shaking. It wobbled to the left, then to the right and miraculously righted itself.

Mother began to pace again. Her hands flailed in the air as if she were erasing the racers, tourists, and summer residents.

"I hate the tourists that overtake our island in the summer!"

Father got up, put his hands on her shoulders and gently squeezed.

"They are only here for the summer, lovey. I am sorry we had to sell the acreage. Think of the jobs the resort and camping area brought for our residents. And besides, we were able to keep the house."

Why do we all try to calm her? I thought angrily. We should let her drown in her own hostility! The trouble is she would probably pull us all down with her. I reached over to spoon some raspberry jam on my plate, careful not to clatter against the crystal bowl or spill on the tablecloth. Success! I released a small puff of air in relief. Father glanced at me covertly and winked.

"Do you want to take a drive somewhere, out of this racket?" Mother's reply was cutting.

"Not if we have to take the children."

Father grimaced as if being stung, then quickly settled his face to impartiality to hide his feelings from me, I knew.

As usual, he turned a blind eye to Mother's cruelty. He capitulated.

"Might not be a good idea, at any rate. The traffic will be fierce."

I recognized the expression on my father's face. It was a taut mixture of conciliation, anxiety, and sympathy for me. It didn't help me though. At that time I couldn't understand why he didn't defend me. *Why doesn't he see what is so plain?* I thought. *Why does he always have to back down?*

Father was holding Mother's anger at bay. He was the omnipresent pacifist in our household.

Once my plate was empty, I asked, "May I be excused?"

Mother rang the small iron bell beside her plate to summon Anna, who stood a short distance down the hall. She entered the dining room in silence, well aware that trouble was brewing. She did her best to stay under Mother's radar on days like this.

I glanced at Father while Mother was busy watching Anna. He nodded without a sound and motioned for me to leave quickly while Mother was sidetracked by Anna's activity.

I slipped out of my chair, slid it back carefully under the table and then stole away. Once out of the room, I quickly ran up the stairs to my bedroom on the second floor and shut the door firmly, relieved to be out of the centre of the tornado downstairs.

My bedroom overlooked the lake. The ceiling sloped down, so I had a storage area under the roof. That's where I kept all my secret notebooks. I loved to write stories. I also hid my diary there. Father painted my room a light blue and drew clouds of white on the walls. Photos were tucked around my mirror frame on my white dresser. A photo of Sally, our black spaniel, was amongst them. Another photo was of our family in a rowboat at Big Bear Lake. Times were good then, before Father got sick. Mother was happy then, too.

The air in my room was hot and motionless. I raced over to the window and shoved it open wide. A slight breeze blew in from the lake. I caught a glimpse through the trees of the speedboats racing at breakneck speed. Plumes of water sprayed behind them. The smell of gasoline and acrid smoke filled the air.

Disappointment lodged hard as a stone in my belly and settled there. I was angry at myself as well as my mother. I learned early not to count on things. It hadn't made me immune to hope, though. I quickly pulled my diary out from its hiding place under my bed. I scrambled for my pen in my white dresser drawer and scribbled my thought for the day: *Don't count on things, ever!* I hastily grabbed my binoculars and pulled them over my neck. I raced down the staircase, two at a time, and quietly slipped out the side door to the ancient leafy black walnut tree next to our carport.

I pulled myself up to the crook of the giant tree, too quickly. My knees scraped against the rough bark, paring the skin off my bare knees. They began to sting badly and burned red hot, throbbing painfully. I settled myself into the bowl of the tree. I studied the droplets of blood bubbling up from the scratches for a few minutes, waiting for the pain to subside. I lay back into the bowl of the tree and closed my eyes. I thought of times when Mother was not ill, and things were better. I felt the rough, creviced bark of the tree. I felt a comforting connection. I could feel the life and pulse under my hand.

The sound of roaring engines broke into my thoughts. Excited announcements blared from a megaphone as the boats rounded the bend. I soon forgot about my wounds. I brought the binoculars up to my eyes and adjusted the focus. I started to concentrate on the race as the boats charged past.

I looked from my leafy perch down the lane to the main road. Traffic was backed up on the way to the resort and 'Dog Patch,' the property Mother sold to accommodate the summer cabins, roughly built A-frames and campers. There was an onslaught of weekend renters coming to watch the races. A snake of RVs, cars, and trucks moved in a steady stream up the asphalt road. A cacophony of sounds assaulted the island's usual peacefulness. Radios blared. Loud laughter rang out from the cars' open windows. Car horns beeped. Young boys whooped and hooted in ear-splitting repetition, echoing each other over and over.

The loud invasiveness of the squealing megaphones worried me. How would Mother handle the relentless grinding engines of the cracker box boats? I felt my stomach begin to churn. Who was going to bear the brunt of her anger this time? Likely me. I was the easiest target.

The soft click of the screen door startled me. Was it Mother? I leaned back into the tree trunk, out of sight. I turned my head slowly and peeped through the thick branches. It was only my older sister, Erin, also sneaking out.

I leaned over and whispered, "Where are you going? Are you going to see that Raymond again?"

Erin looked steadily at me, pondering her reply. She looked set to bolt. I felt an urgent need to talk to her before she took off.

I whispered, "Father will be upset if he sees you with that old guy!"

Erin turned to face me and said, "He won't know I am seeing Raymond unless you tell him."

I felt compelled to make her stay.

"What will I say if he asks?"

"Nothing. You didn't see me, okay?"

"Mother said you couldn't date until next year."

"You never saw me, okay? Jeez!"

Erin quickly turned away from me then darted off down our dusty gravel lane. Her blonde ponytail swung back and forth behind her as she flew toward the main road. Small arcs of dust and pebbles of gravel spurted upwards as her white bucks hit the lane. Her blue sleeveless dress was short, exposing long, tanned legs. A shell necklace bounced against her neck.

I pulled my binoculars up to my eyes again to watch her speed down the lane. Raymond was waiting near the door of his red jeep. He eyed Erin as if she were prey as she sprinted down the lane. A sudden bolt of fear ripped right through me. I shuddered.

I was hurt by the sudden distance Erin had placed between us lately. I suspected Raymond was to blame for it. Raymond wore the same old outfit he always wore. An old, greasy, felt cowboy hat covered his long, oily, grey hair. His ancient, fringed, suede vest covered his pale blue cotton shirt. His jeans were soiled and ragged. A heavy gold chain hung from his neck. He wore scruffy cowboy boots. The sun glittered off his sunglasses. The polarized lenses hid his eyes. Never did you see him without his beast of a dog. The German shepherd sat at strict attention by his side, his long tongue dripping gobs of white saliva lolled out of the side of his mouth. His ears laid straight back. His black eyes pierced Erin in a fixed stare.

Once Erin reached the jeep, Raymond motioned for her to get into the passenger side quickly. He glanced around to see if anyone was watching and then glimpsed up our lane. Alarmed, I immediately pulled back into the thick branches. A few moments later, I brought the binoculars up to my eyes again for another peek. I saw the dog's eyes follow Erin steadfastly as she slipped into the jeep's passenger seat. With a whistle, Raymond signaled the dog. I watched as the dog bounded swiftly onto the back seat behind Raymond. Raymond turned his head suddenly and took a quick look up the lane again. I swiftly pulled the binoculars back down and hid once more behind the thick branches.

After a few short moments my curiosity got the best of me. I drew the binoculars back to my eyes. I watched Raymond hurriedly jump into the driver's seat, watched as he waited for the traffic to slow and then watched him deftly take advantage of an opening to maneuver the jeep into the right lane. In a back-spew of gravel, tires spinning, motor squealing, they tore off, making their escape.

Like an omen, a dark cloud appeared out of nowhere and covered the sun. I envisioned my family shattering like glass into a thousand pieces right before my eyes.

I climbed down from my tree, ran into the garage, hopped onto my bicycle and raced down to the acres of A-frames, tents and RVs situated in our old acreage. I learned to become invisible when Mother was in one of her terrorizing rages. When her hurricane force fury materialized on the horizon, we all quickly removed ourselves from her path.

I often went to Dog Patch to hide and think things through. There was a sandy beach there where I liked to read and write stories.

At the Dog Patch steel gate I got off my bike and walked it

down towards the beach, past the cabins and A-frames, towards the small grocery store installed in the complex for the summer residents that lived there. When I reached the store, I noticed the young man I had seen earlier hopping in his bare feet on the blistering tarmac between his parents' cars. He was a gangly boy, with hair the color of wheat, curly, like a lamb's. He was sitting on a bench on the verandah. He watched me curiously. His shoulders were slumped backward, resting against the wall. His lanky legs distended in front of him, crossed sloppily at his ankles. He wore high-top Nikes, no socks. His sunglasses were perched on his forehead.

I was thirsty. I wanted a Coke. I had change in the pocket of my green- and yellow-striped pedal pushers. I slid past him hurriedly, head down, certain that my face was crimson red. When I came out of the store, he had gone.

I saw him several times that summer before I eventually spoke to him. On the day that we finally did speak, he was alone at the side of his A-frame. He was bouncing a basketball off the small arc of concrete and tossing it into the basket. I seized the opportunity. It was now or never.

I approached him tentatively.

"Hi! I've seen you around."

He swung around, startled.

"Hi there! My name is Jake. Are you an all-timer?"

"Maddy. Yes, and you're a weekender?"

He tossed the ball onto his A-frame's verandah, then came over to face me.

"You could say that."

I was desperate to keep our conversation going now that I had come this far.

"You're here for awhile, then?"

"We're staying for the entire summer. Dad goes into the city weekdays to work but comes back here during the weekend."

He casually pulled a red package of Matinees out of his shirt pocket and slowly extracted a cigarette. He placed it into his mouth, then searched into his pants pocket and pulled out a red lighter. He lit up his cigarette in a James Dean sort of way, took a long drag and then blew out a circle of smoke. As unexpected and as sudden as a mosquito bite, I was instantly smitten.

I glanced away from him lest he saw my admiration. When I looked away, I noticed my cousin Connor strolling down the gravel road to the store.

I quickly whispered a garbled goodbye, raced to my bike at the store and sped off for home.

All that summer long I worried about Erin's safety. I was also concerned about how Mother and Father would react should they find out that I knew about Raymond all along. I was amazed that Erin wasn't caught yet. Nightly, I prayed fervently that she would get caught so the burden would be off my shoulders. Erin was dreamy and light during this time, blissfully unaware or not caring about the tension that was building up in our household.

FIREWEED ISLAND, FALL 1955

The islanders loved the fall. That year, the sun still had a bite to it. The days were still sunny, with a slight, crisp breeze, a true Indian summer. Best of all, after the tourists retreated to their normal lives in the city, the small island was their own again.

That first Monday after Labor Day, I woke up impatient to get to school. My friend Sally told me on the phone the night before that she had the latest *Seventeen* magazine and that I could read it with her at noon hour. I raced down to breakfast. I was running late, per usual. I was writing in my diary. I forgot the time. Erin was already bent over her breakfast of eggs and toast. Anna must have heard me coming down the stairs. She shuffled in her soft slippers into the dining room with my breakfast the minute I arrived at the table. She appeared troubled.

Erin glanced up at me and then looked quickly away as I sat down. Her eyes were red-rimmed and swollen as though she had been crying for hours. Her long blonde hair was tucked and tangled into the hoodie top she always slept in. It was clear by her disheveled appearance that she had slept badly, if at all. My throat tightened in sympathy as I watched Erin concentrate on every bite she took. I could see that it was all she could do to choke down her food.

I broke the silence.

"Aren't you coming to school on the bus today?"

When I looked at Erin's face, I could see the panic and uncertainty that pulled her down. Her reply was muffled.

"No—going in with Mother later."

I became alarmed.

"Why?"

Erin softly replied, "She didn't say. You know her!"

All that long day, I struggled to concentrate during my classes. My attention constantly wandered back to Erin and Mother. At last, the dismissal bell rang and I was able to rush to the waiting school bus. As soon as I stepped in, my eyes swept over the bus like a searchlight seeking Erin's face. She wasn't there. I knew right then that something terrible had happened at home.

The journey home seemed to last for hours. Our old, yellow school bus lingered at each stop sign. It took my friend Henry so much time to get off the bus at his stop that I wanted to strangle him. He was the class clown. He always made a funny exit every day. I wasn't in the mood for his antics today.

At last the school bus dropped me off at the end of my lane. I started to march home quickly. On either side of me, plum trees hung low with an abundance of lush, plump, purple fruit. The sky was darkening fast. A strong wind rippled the grasses in the fields. Suddenly I heard a loud swish of air above me. A whole row of the fruit trees released a spray of silver green leaves cascading to the ground like colorful confetti.

The metallic smell of an approaching storm was in the air. The east wind howled around me. I pulled the collar of my winter coat up to my chin. Strong gusts of wind blew off the lake, licking like fire at the school papers I gripped in my hand. The squall threatened to grab the papers and scatter them all over the fields beside me. I clutched my homework tightly and quickly shoved them any which way into my school case. The papers became crumpled as they brushed against my half-eaten egg sandwich left over from lunch. I knew that the sulfur stink of the eggs would stick to my homework papers, but it was too late to worry about that. All my thoughts were on what I might find when I got home.

Erin's absence on the bus continued to nag me as I continued to trudge up the lane. Trouble was brewing. I could sense it.

I heard the loud honking above before I saw the V of wild

geese flying overhead. I wished I were flying with them, leaving my troubled family.

"No one would miss me," I uttered. I startled myself with my thinking aloud. "I am tired of worrying about everybody in our family!"

I noticed that Father had piled wood in the garage by the side door for the winter. It was a good sign that he was okay. Father's complexion was grey lately. I knew that Mother was concerned about his health. I sensed a new fatigue in Father's manner and heaviness in his steps. He was born with a hole in his heart. He never should have worked in a coal mine. His heart was not strong enough to cope with the added stress.

On top of this, he contracted silicosis from the dust in the mine. His constant coughing worsened his heart condition. Throughout the nights I could hear his ragged breathing coming from his bedroom. These days his furry eyebrows were constantly scrunched up and his face always drawn. His usual good humor was forced. I loved his face when he found something funny. I missed his good humor. His whole face would crumble up into a huge smile. Every day he would teach me a new word and its meaning. He loved to read as much as I did.

As I neared the house I heard heated angry words. My heart began to beat a rat-a-tat drum roll in my chest. I stepped up my gait. As soon as I reached the carport entrance I heard angry voices reverberating against the walls.

I slipped into the mudroom of our house unnoticed. I carefully left the door ajar so they wouldn't hear it shut. I was cold to the bone. I wrapped my coat more closely around me, but the chill remained. A small breeze from the open door curled around my neck. A cold shiver slithered down my spine. My teeth began to shudder.

I slid behind the kitchen door. I put my eye right up to the door jamb to watch the scene unfold before me. From my viewpoint I could make out shadows of Mother, Father and Erin edged against the linoleum floor. I took a chance. I slowly opened the kitchen door a wee bit. Father was pacing. Erin was sitting on a kitchen chair that was pulled away from the table. She sat facing Mother.

Mother was standing very still and glared furiously at Erin. Suddenly, she swiftly marched over to Erin's chair, towering over her.

"Erin," Mother started up again. "How could you disgrace us like this? I will never live it down!"

Erin tried to say something, "I'm sorry", perhaps, or, "It was an accident," or another weak response, but her words collapsed, coming out as a whimper under the pressure of Mother's dangerously close presence.

She growled, "What did you say? Did you say something?"

Erin remained silent. Perhaps this is what caused Mother to snap, the sight of Erin sitting on the chair, protecting her stomach with her hands, protecting her baby and the embarrassment of people knowing about it, knowing that people would talk.

Father made pleading, pacifying responses.

"Florence, it's done! We can handle this! Calm down, please. This is not helping. Erin hasn't done this intentionally to hurt us. It's what Erin wants that counts now!"

Father walked near the door I was hiding behind. I quickly slipped back toward the wall behind me. From this viewpoint, I saw only shadows again. A brief silence filled the space after Father's comments. I feared the worst. What was left in Mother's arsenal? She would not take kindly to any interference from Father.

Without warning, Mother's shadow loomed over Erin again. I edged back to the door frame again to obtain a better view.

Erin suddenly stood up from her chair. She roared in protest.

"I won't give up my baby! You can't make me!"

"I can, and I will!" Mother's shadow neared perilously close to Erin's shadow.

Father tried to wedge himself between the two of them but was too late. Lightning swift, Mother's hand struck Erin's cheek with such a brute force that Erin's head snapped back violently.

"God's sake, Florence," Father said tersely. "That's enough now!"

Erin's face contorted. Her words came out in a piercing screech.

29

"I hate you!"

She thrust Mother aside and shot out of the room. She pushed the door back with such strength that it smashed against my shoulder. I winced in pain. I clenched my mouth shut to prevent myself from crying out.

Erin dashed up to her bedroom, slamming the door with a thunderous thud. The blast bounced off the walls. The hall mirror quivered. The ornaments of the table trembled beneath it. A split second later there was an eerie stillness.

Mother did not follow her to make peace as I had hoped. Erin brought shame to the good name of our family. I knew that would never be forgiven. I retreated to my own bedroom, shutting the door firmly behind me. An unnatural stillness hung over the house like a soft blanket. No one made a move to patch things up, stifling any chance to reconcile.

I darted to the garage and pulled out my bike, racing down my usual route down the plum tree lane and then down past the fields to Dog Patch. I needed to remove myself from the stifling containment at home. I missed Jake. He had returned to Vancouver with his family and seldom got to borrow his father's car to come out to see me. I was surprised to find the front gate tightly secured with a large metal chain and a lock. I decided to trespass. I leaned my bike against the gate and hopped over the chained metal fence. As I walked down the tarmac towards the lake, a stiff breeze stirred the leaves of the maple trees. The air was blessedly cool and damp. Leaves whirled in a kaleidoscope pattern of red, yellow and green and shed like colorful confetti to the ground.

I glanced at Jake's cabin as I strolled toward the lake. The house had a desolate look about it. The windows of his family's A-frame were woven with spider webs. The cheerful blue checkered curtains were drawn tight. The porch swing where Jake and I spent many hours talking was stored away somewhere.

Further along the complex, I passed the little grocery store that was installed there for the use of the summer residents. The window of the snack counter was blocked off with plywood. In the sandbox nearby a child had left a little blue plastic pail and a bright yellow shovel near a mound of sand. The swings were pulled up and secured with chains. The scene was a reminder of happier times, and it made me even more morose.

I settled myself underneath a huge yellow willow tree that bent towards the lake. The lake was shallow. Frogs sang in the swampy bottom. A pair of swans drifted across the surface of the lake like sailboats in tandem. The sun, which had shined anemically all morning, slithered behind murky clouds. Despair hung over me like the thick threatening clouds that were accumulating above.

FIREWEED ISLAND, NOVEMBER 1955

During the weeks that followed, Erin and I spent much of our time in our bedrooms. We both felt far removed from the activities below us. Mother and Father could be heard having heated arguments at the kitchen table. Mother's high-pitched strident voice overrode Father's soft, firm tone.

A few weeks after Erin's confession, Father and Mother took a mysterious trip to Vancouver. When they returned, it appeared that a truce had been formed between them. Mother was unusually cheerful throughout our dinner the evening they returned from Vancouver. She asked Anna to bring out their best wine. Father was subdued and uncomfortable. He kept tugging at his shirt collar as if it was strangling him. Often, he would look off in the distance during our dinner as if to remove himself from what was going on at the table. None of us knew how to act when Mother was like this. Her gaiety was tinny and brittle and as false as fake jewelry. When we finished our dinner and Anna removed our plates, Mother's mood swiftly changed.

She stood up from the table and looked straight at me.

"Go straight to your room and don't linger."

"What did I do?" I whined.

"I'll call you down when we're through."

This remark scared me.

"Through with what?"

"Don't be nosy, girl. Get going!" Her hands brushed the air, shooing me away.

I left quietly and slid behind the kitchen door. I had a strange sense of déjà vu. I feared for Erin's safety.

This time, though, I was thwarted. Mother quickly stepped to the door I was hiding behind. She grabbed my shoulders roughly, spun me around, and thrust me toward the staircase, kicking my heel, shooing me out like she did to our cat when she was underfoot.

"Your sneakiness will get you into trouble, my girl!"

I felt a hot pressure in my throat, not tears, but bitterness and rage, blinding white rage. I was helpless to help Erin.

I stormed up to my bedroom to wait for the explosion that was bound to come. But all remained mute. The house was like a tomb that evening. I kept to myself in my bedroom. I read until exhaustion overtook me. Not knowing what occurred downstairs that evening terrified me.

Once I heard our parents retire, I snuck down for a glass of milk and snatched some cookies from the glass jar on the kitchen counter. The house was hushed. The kitchen looked forsaken and jumbled. Mother's and Father's wineglasses stood unrinsed on the kitchen counter. Bits of hard yellow cheese and thin twigs of grapes lay curled on a small green plate. Erin, Father, and Mother were all sleeping soundly. Had they all become accustomed to the chaos?

The next morning while I was in the kitchen preparing a jam sandwich for my school lunch, Erin slowly shambled in, dragging her feet. It was Anna's day off. Her unbrushed hair fell in clumps around her pale face. Her head hung low as if a huge weight were laid upon her shoulders. She wasn't wearing her usual nightwear. She was wearing the clothes she had on yesterday, and it was clear that she had slept in them.

I attempted to cheer her up.

"Do you want me to make a jam sandwich for you, too?"

Erin mumbled. "Not necessary, I won't be going."

"Why not?" I asked.

At that moment, Mother bustled into the kitchen full of purpose and in full control. She was wearing her best blue dress. Her hair was curled back off her face and pulled into a neat bun. She was wearing makeup and her navy blue heels.

Mother moved toward me.

"Maddy, get a move on. I am driving you to school today."

"It's too early. Can't I wait for the school bus? I will have to wait outside until it opens! What about Erin? Is she coming too?"

"Do as you're told for a change! Do you have to question everything I say? Get going!"

Mother walked to the garage, opened her car door and started the ignition, then waited for me impatiently. I took one last glance at Erin, picked up my lunch box and got into the idling car. We were silent during the entire drive to school. I felt desperate to ask what was happening, but I knew it was futile to ask. I would have to be patient and wait and see.

When we got to the school, I got out and stood on the curb. I waited for her to say something, anything.

She looked into her rearview mirror to see if traffic was coming and said over her shoulder, "If I am not home after school, start your homework. Anna will be there this afternoon."

Two other kids were also waiting at the door, shivering in their thin jackets. Both of them were from the trailer park, and they kept to themselves. It would be awkward to stand beside them until the door opened. They put their backs to me when I started up the stairs to the door. They began to whisper and laugh outrageously at a joke they had just shared, looking over their shoulders and snickering at me. Finally, the janitor opened the door, and my school day began.

Erin wasn't on the bus again that afternoon. I was worried sick. When the bus dropped me off, I rushed up the lane. Our car was parked in the carport. Wherever they had gone, they were back.

I opened the door softly then slipped into the house. The kitchen was empty. I walked down the hall to the living area. I heard soft classical music coming from the den. I found my parents sitting silently in the living room. Father was sitting in his easy chair, staring into space. He was nursing a glass of Scotch, rolling the liquid around the ice cubes. When he heard me come into the living room, he glanced up at me. He was still wearing his best blue suit and his navy tie with his gold clip. Guilt etched his drawn face.

He spoke tentatively.

"Erin's gone for a wee holiday, lovey."

I waited for an explanation, but there was none forthcoming.

"Dad?" I willed him to say more.

Father's eyes turned to Mother. She got up quickly from the sofa and picked up her teacup from the coffee table.

"No more discussion, Maddy. Make yourself some tea. Take it up to your room, and do your homework. Anna will call you down for dinner."

My stomach somersaulted, but I did as I was told, not knowing where Erin was or if she was okay. Questioning Mother now would make things worse.

I found out from Father later in the evening when Mother was bathing. Erin was sent to the Salvation Army Home for Unwed Mothers in Vancouver. Erin was told that she must give up the baby. I knew Erin wanted to keep her baby. I wondered what Mother threatened her with.

Mother told me that Erin was not allowed visitors. This would have been Mother's decision, not the home's. I was sure of that. The die was cast. All of our family obeyed Mother's ruling. No one dared bring up Erin's absence. It was as if she never existed.

FIREWEED ISLAND, CHRISTMAS 1955

Christmas Eve morning Father gave me the news: we would be spending Christmas with Erin in Vancouver. My parents rented a motel room for Christmas Eve and Christmas Day. Erin was allowed to leave the home for two days. I couldn't wait to see her again. We were to leave just as soon as Mother got home from work.

I sat at the round oak kitchen table as Father packed cardboard boxes of special treats for our Christmas dinner: homemade mustard pickles, canned shrimp, pickled onions, homemade pickles, Christmas candies, soft gummy fruit slices, chocolates, and Father's favorite, sugared ginger slices.

I looked at the clock, five p.m. The sun was setting in the west. The white snow frosting on Devil's Mountain across the lake was tinged a light pink. The clouds that hovered above were traced in orange and green. Stiff whitecaps skipped across the dark green lake. An east wind was building up.

I put my hand on my father's shoulder and hugged him from behind. The comfort was more for me than him. I was nervous. I was so afraid that Mother would change her mind once she got home. Father pulled up his arm and patted me on my shoulder to reassure me but continued filling the boxes. He knew I was worried about the predicted storm.

I peered outside.

"Father, it looks like snow."

Father glanced up.

"Likely it will, pumpkin."

Startled, I said, "We'll still go? Erin will be so disappointed. She can't miss Christmas!"

Now Father looked straight at me.

"We'll get there, lovey, not to worry, now."

I sighed deeply, and Father laughed at me lightly. My stomach growled. I was hungry. I am always hungry when I am nervous. I walked over to the kitchen counter and pulled some bread out of the bread keeper on our kitchen counter. I offered some to Father, but he waved it away, intent on getting the boxes packed.

Suddenly, the room darkened as if a light switch had been turned off. Evergreen branches beside the dining room window brushed and scratched shrilly against the window panes. The east wind began to howl, shrieking around the house. Mother was paranoid over the wind. Perhaps it was because it was something she couldn't control. She would put her hands over her ears and pace during a wind storm.

At last I heard Mother's little Austin chugging bravely up the lane. I swiftly yanked my black and white wool Indian sweater off the hall rack and pulled it on to wait for her in the garage. I watched the headlights bounce up and down, reflecting the first falling of feather-like snowflakes. They swirled in kaleidoscopic patterns in the headlight's golden orb.

When Mother's car finally reached the garage, she stepped out slowly, looking tired and weary.

I tried to be cheerful.

"Hi, Mother. We're all packed, nearly!"

Mother spoke quietly. This was unusual for Mother.

"Make me tea, Maddy, and then we'll go."

By the time they finished their tea and Father had packed up the car, the storm was raging. Large snow drifts began to form in huge humps on the lane.

Father pulled Mother's coat off the rack and held it out to her.

"We'd better get a move on if we are going to get out of here."

Mother turned to face me.

"Get your coat on, Maddy. Just put the dishes in the sink and leave them."

I clambered into the back seat of the car, stepping over the boxes that Father had placed there. Mother sat like a stone in the front seat, her face impassive. Father slowly reversed the car out of the garage. He gradually turned the car to the right to enter the lane. Without warning, our car spun sideways out of control.

Father cursed softly under his breath and then spoke louder.

"I went too fast, sorry."

Mother placed her hands firmly on the dash, face taut, eyes tightly shut. She drew in a huge mouthful of air then exhaled slowly.

Father righted the car, and we proceeded to chug down the lane. The snow was falling so thick we could hardly see more than a foot ahead of us. Huge gusts of strong wind blew snowflakes erratically over the fields. Already, there was a buildup of snow on the wooden fence beside our lane. As I sat back quietly and watched Mother, I began to feel uneasy. It was very possible she might force Father to turn back home.

The east wind shook our small car as if it were a toy matchbox car while we stumbled ahead, agonizingly slow through the large snow drifts accumulating on our lane.

The snow plummeted down steadily. The wind raged, pulling and pushing the flakes in a strange manic pattern. Snow eddied across the open fields beside us and down the unpaved length of our lane.

Father peered through the windscreen, his nose almost on the window pane.

"Florence, I can't see where the road is." The car was fogging up inside. Father opened his side window and then swiped at the outside windshield with his gloved hand. Our windshield wipers swept back and forth fiercely, failing to keep up with the relentless cascade of heavy snow. We plodded forward, inch by inch. The air in the car was as cold and bitter as an icebox.

"We must keep going. If we stop, we're finished," Father said tersely.

All at once, our Austin swerved sharply to the right, sliding into a small ditch. *This is it,* I thought. *We're finished.* Father gunned the motor. The car didn't move an inch. He reversed the gears to back out of the ditch so we could gain some leverage to pull us up to the lane. The car eased back then stopped. We hit a rock. Father shifted gears again. We moved forward a foot and then slipped right back into the ditch. While the car was still, the snow continued to flow down the icy windshield, disappearing and appearing with each determined swipe of the wiper blade. Now that the window was open, I felt so cold that I started to shiver. I could see my breath in the car.

"Florence, you drive, and I'll get out and push," Father said as he slipped out of the car. Mother reached over to the steering wheel with her hands, pulled herself over the gear box and dropped into the driver's seat.

Father began to rock the little car back and forth gently.

"Florence, gun it!"

The car spurt ahead suddenly and then we were on the lane again. Father struggled up the little slope. He slipped twice before he made it up to our lane. The snow fell into his boots and soaked his pant legs. He shuddered as he crawled into the car. Once we got onto the main road, it was clear sailing.

We arrived in Vancouver in record time. We were all so relieved to reach the motel. There were individual small cabins with a small lawn in the front. Each had an evergreen wreath on the door with a large red and white candy cane attached to it. The cabins looked cheery.

I saw the curtains part as we walked up the steps to our cabin. Erin was peeping out the front window. Once she saw us she raced to the door and opened it quickly to greet us. Her tummy was huge. She was shaped like a pear. Her clothes were clean and pressed. Her blonde hair was pulled back in neat French braids. I hugged her tightly, breathing in the lemony scent of her hair. When I released her, I saw that her forced removal from our small family had taken its toll. She looked so fragile. She looked as if she could break, her face wan, her back stiff.

Once all the boxes were brought in from the car, and the food was put in the small bar fridge in the kitchen, we were able to relax. I knew that everything was going to be all right then. After Erin had the baby and had given it up, we could go on with our lives. Hopefully, Erin could live with this decision, and Mother would forgive her in time.

Erin handled Mother differently than I. She had stopped hoping for any closeness when she was still little, and she became impassive in defense.

We were just getting settled when Father slipped out to the car again. It appeared he didn't want us to see him leave. I pretended I didn't see him. As soon as he closed the door behind him, I raced to the side window and stole a look to see where he was going. He approached our car on the curb in front of our cabin and from the boot of the car he pulled out a mysterious looking parcel. It was long and wrapped in brown paper. I couldn't tell what it was.

When he pulled open the front door, he held the parcel with his left hand behind him. He asked us all to close our eyes tight. We heard the brown paper being pulled off the parcel carefully. Then we heard a tinkle sound.

"Okay, open up!" He shouted with glee.

He had placed a small Christmas tree on the side table with a small set of twinkling white lights and a small white and gold angel on the top.

We had a great time! There was no mention of Erin giving birth shortly or anything about her decision to give the child up for adoption. The subject was not touched. Father tried very hard to keep things cheerful. Mother was strangely quiet and subdued. The two days flew by without incident. We went for long walks and stopped for coffee and hot chocolate at cafes along the way.

FIREWEED ISLAND, JANUARY 1956

After that weekend, Erin made the shocking decision to keep the baby and to live with Raymond. This news destroyed Father. He realized Erin would be completely lost to us then. He became subdued and morose. He spent a good deal of time in the toolshed tinkering with the tractor engine or just sitting there looking into space. Mother looked defeated and drawn. Father and I both noticed, however, that her rage was quietly bubbling, volcanic like, under the surface. Father and I became tense, the earth reverberating beneath us, waiting for the eruption to occur. Her mood could change lightning swift from a dark, sad place to a light, giddy place, then to an angry, murky place again in short order. It was as if she were possessed and could not control the voices within her head.

Just as disturbing to me, Father was coughing almost all night long. I would hear him get up during the night and pace. He would go to the kitchen and get some cold water out of the jug in the refrigerator, pour it into a tall glass and swallow it all down as if he were parched. His throat must have been raw from the continual unrelenting coughs.

One morning after another long night of Father's coughing and pacing, I approached Mother about it.

"Mother, can't we do something for Father's coughing? He hardly slept."

Mother put her teacup down and faced me.

"Don't talk to him about his coughing or his getting up during the night! He hates to have pity for it. Do you understand?"

"I wasn't! I just wondered, could we help him with it? Has he seen the doctor?"

I waited for her answer, but none was forthcoming.

"Maddy, eat your breakfast and never mind."

She frowned at me with disapproving eyes. Angry lines pulled the corners of her mouth down. I hated Mother then, dismissing me, excluding me. I only wanted to help.

The subject was closed. I was left out of everything. I wasn't allowed to mention Erin, either. That subject was taboo also.

FIREWEED ISLAND, FEBRUARY 1956

Father announced that he and I were going to pick up some lily bulbs that he ordered from a shop in Chinatown in Vancouver. Just the two of us were going.

Father and I set out in high spirits. After we drove for a few miles, we stopped at a small grocery store by the side of the highway to buy Cokes. From there, we drove a little further and pulled off the highway to stop at a scenic outlook over the Fraser River. Father parked the car. Then we walked over to a picnic table and sat sipping our drinks quietly for awhile. The scene below provided a breathtaking view of the rushing green-brown water of the river.

Father finished his Coke then lit up an illicit cigarette. His doctor forbade him to smoke, but he often snuck one when Mother was not around to nag him about it.

He pulled in a huge drag, let it out slowly, and said, "Maddy, I know you miss your sister. Be patient. We'll sort things out. You will see."

I very much wanted to believe him. It gave me a glimmer of hope that our family might survive after all.

The river below rushed madly downstream to join the ocean. The local fishermen and the native Indians were enjoying a huge salmon run that year. We watched in silence as we saw that more than twenty fishing boats had cast their nets in wide arcs.

We gazed at the fishermen silently for awhile, content to be still in the warm, soothing pine-scented air. Bees hummed out of tune nearby in a lilac tree behind us. The sun, strong on our backs, relaxed us.

Father soon spoiled our contentment.

He got up hastily then said, "Let's go. It's getting late."

He was quiet and distracted as we drove the fifty miles to the city. I noticed that his complexion was grey, and his eyes looked pained and tired. Once we entered Vancouver, we wound our way through the traffic to Chinatown. We found the florist shop. Father pulled over to the curb and parked across the street from the shop. Father pulled a hanky out from his pants pocket then wiped the perspiration from his brow. His face was now a ghastly grey. The bluish tinge on his lips frightened me. He struggled to pull his wallet out of his jacket pocket. Beads of perspiration traced his brow.

"Dear, run across the street and pick up the plants. Mr. Chan has them ready for us. Take my wallet with you."

Once I crossed the street I glanced back to the car. Father was slumped over the wheel, resting. I was disturbed. Father used to be so full of life. Lately he looked limp, rumpled and exhausted, as if he had just got up from a long restless night with little sleep.

Mr. Chan was involved with another customer when I came in, but he looked up at me and smiled. I started to walk down the aisles and look at all the flowers and plants that were there. I lost myself in the different scents and colors. I was disappointed that Father was not there with me. He loved this store. Last year, we took our time, and Father explained all the plants to me and recited their Latin names.

Just as I started to get impatient, Mr. Chan was free. He shuffled over to me in his blue embroidered silk slippers. He was a small man with a wide, engaging smile. He wore a light blue shirt over soft khaki cotton pants.

"Where your dad?"

"He's in the car."

Mr. Chan looked puzzled.

"He in the car?"

Every year, he and father enjoyed a cup of tea together and took great pleasure in a long conversation about plants. I know father looked forward to it every year, and I suspected Mr. Chan did too.

"I don't think he's feeling well." I said this hesitantly because Father didn't like sympathy. He wouldn't want Mr. Chan's pity.

Mr. Chan hurried past me to the shop window. I saw him look across the busy street to our car. He and I both saw Father slumped over the steering wheel at the same moment. Mr. Chan ran out the door and scampered across the street, sliding deftly between the fast approaching cars coming in both directions. I gasped when I saw a car brush dangerously close, barely missing him.

I watched as Mr. Chan put his nose up to the window of our car. He put his small hand through the open window and placed it on Father's neck. A few seconds later, he twirled around, dodged cars again on his return and then ran past me again to the telephone on the counter. His little brown face was screwed up like an old walnut. Sweat poured down his brow.

He pulled out a white hanky from his pants pocket and wiped his temple.

"Maddy, sit over there. I am going to call for an ambulance for your father."

Mr. Chan started to speak excitedly.

"Come quick to my store, 1025 Yew Street, hurry up, please!"

He listened to the party on the other end and then replied, "Yes, but shallow."

Then I heard, "No blood on face. Slow breathing. Hurry up now."

He put the receiver down and came over to me.

"Maddy, sit here. Don't move. I will go see your father all right. Do not follow, please."

Mr. Chan looked very grave. I watched as he rushed over to the intersection, waited impatiently for the light to change, and then crossed the street to our car.

When I heard the ambulance arriving, I disobeyed Mr. Chan. I ran to the window to watch what was happening to Father. As soon as the ambulance stopped, the ambulance attendants raced to the car and yanked the car door open. I watched as the two men pulled Father gently out of the vehicle and lay him on a stretcher. They quickly placed an oxygen mask on his face and wheeled him to the ambulance.

I ran out to go with him, but a strong hand held me back firmly. I stopped breathing for a moment. I was so scared. People had gathered to watch the action. The ambulance driver and the medic shut the back doors of the ambulance and then shut the passenger doors. They sped away, sirens screaming, to where, I did not know.

I felt faint. Mr. Chan held my head and gently pushed it down, telling me to breathe. Slowly, I felt the blood rise to my head again. When I pulled my head up, Mr. Chan took me back to his shop. He took me to the back rooms where he lived. I felt I was watching a movie as he made me some tea. I wrapped my cold hands around the small blue and white cup without handles. The warmth and the aroma of the strong, sweet tea slowly brought me back to reality. My heart began to beat at a normal pace.

Mr. Chan seemed to sense that I was feeling better. He watched me carefully.

"Any relatives in Vancouver, Maddy, I can phone?"

"Aunt Helen, I guess."

I had memorized Aunt Helen's phone number the last time Erin and I visited her. We were allowed to go to the movies alone in the city, and we were to telephone her when we arrived at the theatre and when we were returning to her house.

Mr. Chan wrote down the telephone number on a small note pad he had in his shirt pocket.

As he was going into the shop to phone Aunt Helen, he said over his shoulder, "Stay there, please, Maddy."

Aunt Helen caused a stir when she bustled into the shop a short time later. She walked straight to me, striding right past Mr. Chan without acknowledging him.

"Maddy, why did the ambulance take your father to Mission, not to Vancouver hospital?"

I would only understand the impact of that statement in retrospect. It turned out that Aunt Helen's comment would haunt me for years. *It was my fault Father died.* The vicious tone of her voice surprised me.

I mumbled a reply, "I don't know."

Mr. Chan noticed my distress and interrupted.

"We didn't know where they were taking him. They not say. They take him away, quick!"

"Come with me then, Maddy." She spun around and started to walk out the door.

I started to thank Mr. Chan, but Aunt Helen interrupted.

"Hurry, Maddy, this is not the time to dawdle."

Aunty Helen embarrassed me, dismissing Mr. Chan as she did. But when I looked back at him over my shoulder, he smiled and nodded his head encouragingly.

The next morning the telephone was ringing as I walked down the staircase from my bedroom to the kitchen for breakfast. I heard the swift scrape of a kitchen chair. Mother must have been rushing to answer it.

As I entered the kitchen, I saw her yank up the receiver and hold it to her ear.

"Yes."

The room went deathly silent. I watched as Mother's body stiffened. She let out a small wail and then dropped the receiver as if it were hot ice. She left the long black cord dangling. She walked away from the telephone as if it were a venomous snake. I went over to place the receiver back on its hook, then I walked over to comfort her, but she shrugged me away. She went to her bedroom and softly shut the door. The telephone immediately rang again. It was the hospital social worker, asking if Mother was all right. She told me to phone one of Mother's sisters right away.

I telephoned Aunt Beatrice next door and told her, "Father's passed." She said she would come right away.

I crept away to my bedroom to process what happened and keep out of the way. I lay on the bed and tried to rest. Whenever I closed my eyes, the reel image of Father spooled back. He was slumped over the steering wheel of his car. Father was dead. It might be my fault. If the ambulance went to a Vancouver hospital, he may have lived. My attic bedroom was hot and airless. I felt sweaty, sticky and lightheaded. My stomach somersaulted over and over. I plopped back onto my stomach and lay motionless to try to stop my stomach from roiling. I tried to think of anything else but what had happened. The scene of Father being rolled into the ambulance kept playing over and over in my head.

The day of Father's funeral was bitterly cold. Not only that, but we were experiencing a freak, strong snowstorm, unexpected so late in the season.

After a small service at the funeral parlor, we followed a black hearse to the cemetery. The cemetery was situated atop a small mountain overlooking the Fraser Valley. The wind propelled the snow in small whirls around us. The snowfall was becoming heavy and thick. The icy snow that slid into my boots startled like an electric shock as I trudged toward the cavernous hole where Father's coffin lay. Mother stood blindly at the gravesite. She was wearing her long fur coat. Around her neck she wore a fox fur scarf. She wore a black felt cloche with netting in the front to hide her face. Her two sisters surrounded her closely as if to protect her from what was happening.

The minister opened his prayer book and began to recite a Psalm, *In the Lord I Put I My Trust.* The wind carried his voice to us in waves, blowing some of his words away into the distance. Although his words swirled around me, I lost the thread of his message. His pearls of wisdom tumbled and plummeted to the ground and crashed like glass beads on a broken necklace. I was deep in the well of grief. I tried to grasp the meaning of the words, but they were out of my reach. We stood over Father's open grave then stepped aside while Mother tossed the first fistful of dirt into the dark pit. My eyes wandered over to the red mahogany coffin. I was sucker punched by the sight. I swiftly turned my eyes away.

Perched on a wooden fence along the highway were three large blue-black ravens, the shiny ebony colors a stark contrast to the surrounding whiteness of the snow. I felt as if I were dreaming.

The ravens started to caw and quarrel amongst themselves. Their breath emitted a tiny puff of fog in the icy air. My mind scratched to bring me back to reality, but I was awake in this dream and I could not escape from it.

I looked back at the priest as he closed his book. People turned back to their cars. Cousin Lily and Mother remained at the grave site. Lily stood still as a statue close to Mother. She let out a sob. Aunt Beatrice was on the other side of her, holding her elbow. I could not get near. I felt shunned, left out in the cold. My eyes searched for Erin, but she was not here. She had not attended the funeral. Whether this decision was hers or Mother's, I do not know.

The ground would freeze soon if this weather kept up. I wondered, *When will they backfill the coffin?* I veered my eyes away again. I turned to face the parking lot behind us.

I walked back to the hearse. Neighbors were huddled there near their vehicles. They talked softly to one another. They soon broke away. It was too chilly to linger. The car doors slammed shut in unison. The roar of their engines revved up. The motors idled softly for awhile to warm the engines. Soon the drivers jumped out of their cars to clear the snow and ice off the windshield. They were surrounded by exhaust fumes. They pulled out stiff cardboard from their wallets or pulled stiff brushes from the back seat to brush the snow off their windows. Ice was beginning to thaw and weep on the glass from the heat of the cars. Then the cars began to pull away slowly in tandem. They snaked down the tarmac road to town.

After the funeral we headed for home. Our car was silent as a tomb. As we pulled into our lane, we saw cars parked up and down the street. There were so many, they spilled all over the yard and under the huge maple trees that grew between Grandma's house and ours. I entered the house through the carport. The house was bursting with people who had brought enough food for a month: casseroles, pies, cold chickens and all kinds of salads. Anna and some neighbors had laid it all out on our kitchen counter.

I eyed a jar of green olives on the counter. I raced over to them. I snapped the lid open in one twist and started eating straight from the jar, using my thumb and index finger. The sticky liquid seeped through my fingers and oozed over my hand and wrist. One after another after another I tossed them down my raw throat until the jar was empty. My hands were sodden, slippery and salty. I licked the juice off my hands then wiped the remainder on my skirt without thought of the consequences.

All afternoon the adults stopped talking whenever I approached. I knew they were talking about my father and what would become of me now. They didn't acknowledge me when I passed by them. It was as if I were not there. Aunt Beatrice and Mother ignored me also, never once asking what I thought or how I felt. I wandered away from them and walked to the stairs up to the bedrooms on the second floor.

Once I heard that everyone had left our house, I stole downstairs to the kitchen. Mother and I were finally alone. I hoped that we could establish some kind of connection now that there was just the two of us left.

I saw that Anna and her crew had packed up all the leftovers and put them neatly in the fridge in containers. The kitchen was spotless. There was not a trace of the crowd that had been there. Mother was in the kitchen. She stood silent and still, her back held ramrod straight. She stared out at the dark, cold lake. It had frozen over since our return from the funeral. We both watched the chilly wind chase little puffs of snow across the ice, each of us held hostage in our own thoughts.

I reached out to her. She brusquely turned away from my attempt at an embrace. She briskly walked away to her bedroom. She shut the door firmly behind her, any hopes of conciliation erased.

I walked into the living room and picked up the afghan off the sofa. I wrapped it all around me, enfolding myself. I fell into the sofa and curled up into a ball, making myself small. I started to think of all the things ahead of me. It began to dawn on me that my life had changed forever. Without my father's protection, I was dangerously vulnerable.

FIREWEED ISLAND, MAY 1956

I suffered great loneliness that year after Father's death. I discovered that you only know your own strength when you learn to keep on loving someone who does not love you back. Mother never let her guard down by showing me any affection. The harder I tried to wrench out some fondness from Mother, the harsher she became.

Jake and I split shortly after. I didn't have the energy it took to maintain a friendship with anyone. This was a decision I have always regretted. I left the relationship without any explanation. I felt a huge guilt. When I matured and grew older, I compared our relationship with all my others over the years, perhaps because I could always remember this as the perfect relationship, perhaps because the first love is always the best. I did know that all my life I would look for him in airports, train stations, on streets.

Those days Mother barely spoke to me. She isolated herself in our house. She paced, smoked and drank behind closed doors. When she emerged, you didn't know what you would be faced with—melancholy? anger? Or would she submerge into a yawning depression?

Shortly after Father's funeral, she returned to work, but as soon as she got home she poured herself a tumbler of Scotch and went straight to the living room while she waited for me to see to dinner.

A few weeks prior to graduation from high school, I was preparing pork chops for dinner on a Thursday evening while Mother was still at work. The chops had been dipped in egg and flour. I had set them on a plate, ready to place them in the skillet once Mother arrived home. Our dog, Tina, whimpered at my feet, and I gave her a piece of carrot. She nibbled at it reflectively. Tina would be ten years old in August. I looked around to see what chores I might have missed before I reached for my homework by the kitchen door. The phone rang. I raced to answer it. It was probably Mother, checking up.

I was nervous. Had I vacuumed properly, made the right thing for dinner? All I needed was for Mother to become stirred up tonight. I had an exam to study for this evening. She would rant and rave for hours and make me too nervous to concentrate on my studies.

I picked up the phone cautiously.

"Hello?"

"It's me, Erin."

"You're home from the hospital? Mother wouldn't let me go see you."

I was so happy to hear from her. I felt sorry for Erin. No one visited her. No one sent her flowers or congratulated her on the birth of her baby.

Erin had a hopeful tone to her voice.

"Maddy, do you want to come see the baby?"

The hopefulness in her voice touched me. I hated to disappoint.

"I can't, sorry."

I twisted the long telephone cord in my hand. I felt horrible. I missed her so much. I was so lonely. The house was like a morgue since Father passed away.

Erin replied quickly, "Raymond can pick you up after school. He will drop you off home before Mother gets home from work next Thursday. She still works late then, doesn't she? She won't even know that you're gone."

I hesitated for only a moment.

"All right, when?"

"Can you come Thursday after school? Raymond will be driving a red jeep. It's a new one. Look for him near the bus stop. Don't tell Mother!"

I hung up quickly. I was afraid Mother might be trying to phone. I would have to explain who I was talking to. Sheer panic invaded me. I hadn't thought it through before agreeing. Mother might phone on Thursday while I was away and find me missing.

On Thursday after school things went through without a hitch. Raymond was waiting for me as planned. As far as I could tell, no one noticed me climb into Raymond's jeep.

The afternoon was sunny. New buds were forming on the trees. Crocuses were peeping out from the gardens as we sped past the housing development near the school. We sped down the highway at top speed. I sat in the passenger seat of the open jeep gazing at the poplar trees in straight formation like soldiers at attention on either side of the highway. Raymond's German shepherd, Kanus, sat at the back, his face high in the air, ears pulled back, nose in the air, enjoying the warm spring breeze, looking ecstatic. He was as calm as I had ever seen him.

I was thirteen. I thought I looked like the tomboy I was. I was still climbing trees, still biking long distances from the island to the dikes with my orange juice and books, content to be on my own.

Neither Raymond nor I spoke for long stretches of time during the journey to Erin's house. Raymond seemed to be very distracted, barely listening to what I said. I was disappointed. I wanted to get to know Erin's boyfriend. I was hoping he wasn't as bad as I thought he was for Erin's sake. He looked straight ahead on the road, barely replying to my questions. I felt edgy, hoping I hadn't made him angry about something.

I didn't know what to expect when we got to Erin's. I imagined that Erin lived in a white house with green trim and a nice garden. I hoped she was happy at last.

Without warning, Raymond made a sharp left turn off the highway. My reverie was interrupted. He made another quick left turn into a lane. It was made almost obscure by gnarled old trees drooping over a rusty gate. You would have to know the entrance was there to notice it. The branches hanging low were eerie. They looked like an old man's arthritic fingers ready to clutch you without warning.

Raymond drove up to an old iron gate, left the jeep idling, and then hopped out. He pulled out some large keys from his jeans pocket. He unlocked the heavy, rusty chains that were wrapped around the corroded gate. He pulled the gate open harshly, causing it to shriek raucously. I jumped out of my skin!

Raymond returned to the jeep. We entered the lane slowly and bumped and twisted around huge potholes until we finally came into a clearing where the house was. I was shocked. The cabin was old and dilapidated. It was in complete disrepair. The screen door was ripped, and its frame was twisted out of alignment like a lopsided grin. The first thing I noticed was that the floorboards on the verandah were uneven, and one of the steps leading up to it was missing. The clapboard siding was peeling. Brown blisters of paint hung on by a thread.

I heard a small cry behind me. It was a goat, loosely roped to a nearby tree. The yard surrounding the cabin was overgrown with twisted blackberry bushes. Underneath lay black plastic garbage bags full of garbage, rusty cans, jars and plastic cups. Scrapes of old metal and corroded farm equipment lay haphazardly around the yard amongst the high blackberry bushes that ran amok.

I felt hugely let down. My dreams of a better life for Erin deflated like a pricked balloon. I was alarmed at Erin's appearance. I hardly recognized her. She was that thin and scrawny. Her eyes were watery and red-rimmed, like a rabbit's. Her hair was dirty and matted. She wore the clothes of a homeless person drifting through life: a long, faded blue skirt, the hemline frayed and grubby above socks sagging over her sandals, the elastic having given up the ghost. Over the skirt she wore a badly stained blouse. A button was missing, causing the blouse to open above her breast.

I gasped and drew back, then quickly recovered, trying hard to hide my disappointment from Erin. Regardless of her circumstances, Erin looked thrilled to see me. I couldn't imagine it. I would be embarrassed to be seen like that.

Erin stepped aside when I reached the porch to let me into the cabin. It was worse than I imagined from the outside. The linoleum on the kitchen floor was so old that it was impossible to determine the original color. The bedroom was just to the left of the kitchen. There was no door to it. Old horse blankets were piled on the unmade bed. The window frames would not keep out the cold. I was sure of that. Dusty, threadbare, frayed blue checkered curtains hung on the window above the kitchen sink. It was filled to the brim with dirty dishes. The fry pan on the greasy stove element was rusted inside. Did they cook in that pan? There was enough dust in the air to choke one.

Regardless of Erin's appearance and living conditions, I was determined to make this visit pleasant. Erin went into the bedroom and brought out Geordie. He was so lovely. I picked him up and inhaled his milky scent. Impulsively, I wanted to run away with him away to a safe, clean place.

Our conversation was stilted as we sat at the small kitchen table. It was weird now to recall how we were when Erin and I were both small. I depended on Erin to save me when we lay hidden under our shared blankets while Mother was in one of her rampages. There were too many topics we had to avoid like land mines. Our lives had diverged into two different paths. I hoped with all my heart that she would be able to find her way back to the family.

Soon, the sun was beginning to set in the west. Through the kitchen window the sun's rays were opaque. Dust and grime prevented any significant light from entering the kitchen. I was becoming anxious about the time. Raymond was outdoors working on the wooden fence surrounding their field.

He came in a few minutes later from his chores wearing muddy boots. He dragged clods of mud in with him. He threw his grimy leather work gloves on the kitchen table. I looked away so he couldn't see my disgust.

I began to feel uneasy. It was getting late. I wouldn't have time to finish the chores Mother set out for me today. That was bound to cause trouble.

Raymond left the room like a shot to go to his jeep. The door slammed loudly behind him. I noticed that he didn't kiss Erin goodbye or even acknowledge her.

He yelled over his shoulder. "I'll be waiting in the jeep. Erin, we're going to Garibaldi Park to test out the jeep on the way home. I might be late getting home."

My heart leapt then somersaulted like an acrobat. *We are going to be further delayed. I'm done for!*

After a hasty goodbye to Erin and baby Geordie, I dashed to the jeep where Raymond was waiting impatiently.

As I pulled myself up to the passenger side of the jeep, I glimpsed Raymond sliding a handgun into the glove compartment. Fear struck me like a lightning bolt scorching my innards. A cold shiver coursed through my whole body, like a dark cloud covers the sun.

I told myself that perhaps he wanted to target practice when we got to the park. I began to feel queasy. I couldn't shake a sense of panic as we drove down the highway towards the park. He was cold and distant during my entire visit. What was going on?

"I can't be late. Mother will be so angry."

He remained closed mouthed and looked straight ahead up the road.

Raymond drove up the highway, turned left at the Haney intersection then sped on to the park. The sun was sliding down behind the mountain peaks. The sky was darkening fast. The jeep began a steep incline on a rough, narrow logging road. Road signs indicated dangerous curves. *Could we pass an approaching logging truck?* My right hand clung to the open window of the jeep, the knuckles stiff and white.

I could feel myself listing forward, the safety belt cutting sharply into my waist as we swerved into the tight corners of the road. Raymond continued to drive farther into the mountains. Every mile thrust up the level of my fear.

Raymond must have read my mind. He broke the silence.

"Don't worry. We won't meet anyone here at this time of the day. Logging has shut down for the day."

All at once, right in front of us, was a huge black bear and her cub. My nerves were on fire! The jeep's top was down. Would the bear attack us to defend her cub? I hoped Raymond wouldn't use his gun. I didn't know what would happen! The black bear sensed us. She turned her massive head around and stared at us for a moment. She swayed her head back and forth and then moved on, the bear cub close behind. We watched as she edged down the steep incline toward the river below. I breathed a sigh of relief. The mother bear kept a close eye on her cub. I felt the closeness and the concern the mother bear had for her offspring. Motherhood should be natural, shouldn't it? Why was my mother so distant? I couldn't understand it.

Raymond fired up the jeep's engine again. Gravel sprayed up behind us as we sped up the road. Up the road a few yards we came upon a wooden bridge that covered a small stream. The jeep came to a screeching halt. A small hurricane of dust blustered behind and around us.

He turned to face me. His face was sinister.

His sharp words startled me.

"Come across or get out!"

I didn't know what he meant, exactly. I looked ahead to the bridge. It looked safe. His words didn't match his tone of voice. I was confused. What was happening?

My thoughts suddenly focused. Instinctively I knew that I had to be alert. We had driven over rough terrain, running creeks and up sharp inclines. Why would he think that I would be scared to go over the bridge?

"What about the bear? Wouldn't we be safer in the jeep?:

Raymond lost his patience with me.

"Get out!"

I hesitated. I heard the glove compartment snap open with a piercing shriek. Metal grated against metal. I chanced a quick glance out of the corner of me eye. He had removed the gun from the glove compartment!

Swiftly, he moved toward me. He thrust the gun against my neck. Ice water coursed through my veins. I was in a cold sweat. My throat was dry with fear.

I barely managed to speak.

"What are you doing?"

Raymond spoke softly.

"Pull down your pants."

I froze. His nonchalance was surreal. He pulled the gun away from my neck and pointed it toward my chest. He then spun the gun carelessly around his index finger. I was terrified that it would accidently fire. I slowly shied away from him. I gradually leaned back to the passenger door. Raymond bent towards me. He placed the gun on my private parts. He grazed it lightly over me. I shivered in terror. He rubbed the gun against my belly and up, over, and around my breasts.

Then, just as suddenly, he moved away from me. I felt a gush of relief. He was just scaring me.

He placed the gun near him on the dash facing me. His eyes never left mine. He lunged toward me again, forcefully ripping my blouse apart with his hands, exposing my breasts. He reached over for the gun, slowly circling my breasts with the nose. Shock immobilized me for a moment or two.

Adrenalin kicked in, enabling me to find my voice.

"Please, stop!"

"Now why would I do that?" His voice was crooning, belying the act.

I forced myself to look at him. His face was contorted with excitement. I had to do something quickly, or I was finished. I needed to escape.

While he was playing with me, I slowly and very deliberately put my right hand behind my back. I groped for the door handle. I found it. Gradually, inch by inch, I pulled the handle down. I could feel a small hesitation in the handle's movement. My hand reached the opening position, so I edged the handle down very gently and very slowly. It clicked open sharply. The sound cut through the silence. It was louder than anything I heard in my life.

Raymond cocked his head. He heard it, too. He seized me back toward him. He held on like a vice. I struggled and twisted away from him. The door was still hanging open. I broke free. I pushed myself against the door. I hurled myself backward and landed on the gravel road. The sharp stones felt like a thousand stinging bees on my back. I strained to get up. Raymond leapt out of his side of the jeep. Kanus dove in behind him.

I hesitated for a second. I had to run to save myself. I ran toward the bridge. I don't know why. My chest burned red hot from exertion. My knees were rubber. Sweat trickled down my chest and back. I stumbled and slipped on the loose gravel, slowing me down. I glanced over my shoulder. I saw that Raymond was still standing in front of his vehicle, observing me run. His gun was in his hand at his side. Kanus was standing at alert a few feet in front of him. He was ready to run and pounce, waiting for a command. Raymond gave me a cursory glance before he jumped back into his jeep.

I was terrified. I didn't know what was going to happen. Was he going to leave me there? Where was the bear? Could I find my way home? It was getting dark and chilly. I began to run again.

I heard his motor rev up in the near distance. The growl of the engine gunned toward me. Should I run or stay? He may be playing a sick joke on me. I started to pray the way our neighbor, Mrs. Cook, taught me at Sunday school.

Instinct told me to run. It was my only chance. He could force me off the road. I could easily slip over the sheer drop to the river. Or he could command his dog to attack me as he drove by. I was on red alert.

He raced past me in his jeep. A few feet ahead, he abruptly braked. Dust flew, surrounding me, choking me. He sat watching me, letting the motor idle. He was going to take me home, after all. It was only a sick joke. I doubled over, queasy with relief.

I would let on it was funny. I would do anything to be safe. He was a sick human being. I'd go along with it.

I limped up to the jeep's passenger door. When my hand reached the door handle he revved up the motor again and sped off. I plummeted to the ground. My back hit the gravel, knocking the breath out of me. Some of the small stones clung to my back as I forced myself to get up. I needed to keep moving. My legs and back were already stiffening with the trauma and the cold.

Raymond's jeep was slowing down a few yards ahead. He stopped near a sightseeing area. There was a small parking area on the left of it. He turned off the motor and got out of the jeep.

A hawk's shrill cry broke the silence. Wind rustled the pine trees. The breeze was welcoming on my sweltering body.

Clearly, Raymond was playing a cat-and-mouse game with me. He held the handgun at his side again. Fear scurried through my veins like a frenzied animal. My hot body became ice cold in a split second.

I knew I was going to be shot. I hoped he would do this quickly to get it over with. I was at a standstill for a brief moment. I gathered up my courage and started to run again. If I was lucky, he would shoot me in the back. I might die quickly.

I felt another flood of adrenalin race through me, enabling me to run swiftly. I didn't feel pain in my legs, chest, or knees. I was flying.

Raymond was gaining on me now. I heard the gravel crunch as his foot fell in close behind me. Oh God! Oh God! His hot musty breath blew on the back of my neck. Then his large hands gripped my shoulders tightly, painfully. He wrenched me back toward him with his left arm. He rammed the nose of the gun to my temple with his right hand and pushed me toward the bushes. He kept pushing me further and further into the forest's thickness.

He kept pushing me with a brute force.

"No one will hear you here, girly!"

Fear swept through me, arctic, immediate.

Raymond gave me one last push. My foot caught on a root of a tree. I fell to the ground so hard and so fast that I bit my tongue. I struggled to get up. Raymond grabbed me by the shoulders and shoved me down to the ground again. He reached down and flung me on my back as if I were a rag doll. My shoulders bounced against the rough terrain, scraping my back.

He reached down again to my jeans waist and started to tug

down brutally. A searing pain ripped through my abdomen, piercing my skin. I remembered that I had hitched my pants together with a safety pin that morning. I had lost my button, and I didn't have time to find another. The pin had popped and it slashed my skin as my pants were shucked down.

Raymond held the gun with his right hand and wrenched his own pants down with his left hand. I glanced down. I had never seen a penis before. It was huge. It shocked me. I pulled my knees up to stop him from coming closer. He slapped my face hard, stunning me. I quickly came to and bit him savagely on his wrist.

He raised his hand to slap me again.

His voice was hard, excited.

"You little hellcat!"

I thrashed about to try to free myself, but he was too powerful for me.

I quickly realized that there was no point in resisting any further. I had to save my strength to survive. I felt a searing pain when he entered me. Raymond's endless thrusting tore right through me. Repulsion for this monster caused burning bile to flow up my throat, threatening to drown me. I felt Raymond's body shudder. He removed himself from me quickly.

"I will kill your sister if you say anything. Understand me?" The threat in his voice was real. I realized when he said that, though, he wasn't going to kill me.

My mind was swimming. I stooped down in a daze to reach for my panties. I saw that they were ripped and useless. They were grass-stained. A splatter of blood was on them. I slipped them into my jeans pocket and got dressed quickly. Goose bumps scattered up and down on my arms like ants on a jam sandwich. I started to shiver uncontrollably.

I managed to limp to the truck. I hurt all over. I was weak and sore. My arms and legs ached. My lungs and throat were scorched and raw. All the way home my hands kept shaking. I placed my hands under my knees to stop the shaking. I looked straight ahead as far as I could see up the highway, willing the miles to speed by to my home, to safety. I was too numb to cry.

Finally, we turned on my island road. He dropped me off at my lane with a final warning.

"I will kill Erin, no problem."

As I staggered up the lane, the image of my house swam like a mirage. Each step didn't seem to put me much closer. My legs felt as if I was treading water knee deep. After what seemed to be an eternity, I finally reached the side door. I stepped inside. We had no locks on our doors. It wasn't necessary. We knew our neighbors and friends, after all. I walked over to the dining room and hauled a chair over to the door. I slipped the chair under the door knob firmly.

I had breakfast dishes to do before Mother got home. There were two or three soggy pink and green Fruit Loops attached to the side of my morning bowl. Mom had left a spoon of jam on her side plate, congealed like blood. I needed to sweep the kitchen also.

I was too sick and too tired to do anything. I limped my way to the sofa in the living room. Surely, Mother would not be angry when she heard what happened. There was a draft coming from our front window. I reached for the old green afghan Mother had knitted a long time ago when she was well. I wrapped it around me tightly. I lay there numbly for awhile until I felt warmer and ceased shaking.

When I shut my eyes, what I started with, what my memory started with, was shutting the side door to my house and pulling a kitchen chair in front of it. The memories suffocated me. I stuffed them down, but they kept coming up to choke.

I needed to get up and get moving. I forced my body out of the shelter of the afghan and stood up. I still ached all over. The sharp pain I felt in my head felt as though someone had hit me over the head with an axe.

I knew that I had to phone the police right away. If I didn't, I knew it would happen again and again. The police would protect Erin and get her away from that monster. I walked over to the phone hanging on the kitchen wall. I pulled the phone book out of the kitchen drawer, found the non-emergency number for the RCMP and then began to dial.

I felt as if someone was watching me. I was startled by a shadow on the wall. I hung up the phone after the first ring. I cautiously stepped up to the window and slowly drew back the curtains a small bit. I couldn't see anyone there. What I saw was just a shadow of tree branches swaying in the breeze. It was a false alarm.

I raced to the phone again. Mother would be home in two hours. I found the non-emergency number again and let it ring through this time.

I started to tell my story to the lady that answered, but I had to stop and back up once in awhile. I was ahead of myself, falling over my words.

Once she understood what happened she interrupted my story and quickly put me through to an officer. I repeated my story again. The officer was kind and put me immediately at ease. He didn't interrupt. I didn't detect a moment of disbelief from him. I had a hard time believing it myself, so I was very relieved when he said he and another officer would be at the house shortly.

I kept watch at the front bedroom window for them. The minutes dragged. Finally, I saw the police car on our main road. He slowed the car at our lane, looked at the number on our mailbox, then swung in. They sped up the lane in a cloud of dust and stopped short in front of our carport.

I waited until they were at the door before I pulled away the chair in front of it. Two officers followed me into the kitchen. Both of them were burly and sort of loped into the room. Mother would be unhappy that I hadn't washed the dishes and cleaned up before they came, but never mind. She might understand. I hoped so.

Their very presence filled the kitchen as they walked toward our round oak kitchen table. One was very tall, and the other was short and stocky. The tall one moved with authority. Both men were middle-aged. The shorter one had a brush cut with streaks of grey. He was solid, not tall. He spoke to me in a gentle voice.

"Please, sit down here with us, Maddy. My name is Officer Kent. My partner here is Officer Charles."

I joined them at the table, still very shaken. I was embarrassed. I didn't know where to look.

I sat with my hands on my lap, focusing my eyes on the pattern on the oilcloth on our table. My legs were shaking. Nerves sent quivers racing up my arms.

"It's not your fault." The older officer spoke softly. I looked up at him. His eyes were almost a non color, grey like the pebbles on our beach. His face was ruddy and weathered. He must have seen a lot of bad things in his work. I felt I could trust him.

"Mother said not to see Erin again. She will be very angry at me."

"You didn't ask for this, Maddy. Your mom will understand."

"No, she won't." The officers were startled by my remark. I caught the officers glance at each other.

Officer Kent pulled his pen from the briefcase and then his yellow legal foolscap pad. He wrote today's date at the top.

"Start from the very beginning, Maddy. Everything you can remember, even the smallest thing."

I quickly got up from the table to remove the dishes and napkins to make room for him to write.

"Sit down, Maddy. Just leave them. Tell us what happened."

They sat at one side of our oak table, and I sat facing them. At some point after I started to relate my story, Officer Kent started to take notes. I started to tell them in spurts, backing up to explain some things, and then moving on with my story. Soon the words were spilling out quickly over and around each other, and I got the account out.

The shorter officer, Officer Charles, interrupted occasionally.

"Could you repeat that for me, Maddy?"

Then he wrote it all down, word for word. They believed me. I could tell.

Officer Kent placed his hand on mine.

"Maddy, can you bring us the clothes you wore, even your underwear?"

I had placed my panties in a paper bag and put them in the waste basket in the bathroom. I excused myself and walked to the bathroom and extracted the ripped, grass-stained panties. I pulled the clothes I had worn that day out of the laundry hamper and returned to the officers. Looking at the floor, I started to hand them over to Officer Kent.

He raised his hand.

"Wait a second, Maddy."

I watched out of the corner of my eye as he pulled out his plastic gloves from his briefcase and pulled them over his huge, beefy hands. He took the panties from me and slid them into a plastic bag and marked the bag with a blue marker. This brought a sense of reality to my nightmare. Finally, someone would take control and protect me and Erin.

I looked up at Officer Kent.

"What about Erin? Will you go get her? She's not safe."

"We'll let you know what happens. First we need to tell your Mother."

My words tumbled out fast. "Can you please leave before she gets home? I will tell her. She frightens easily. If she sees the police car in our garage she will panic. I will tell her, and then you can come. She'll be mad if she sees your car here and is made to worry."

The officers looked at each other as if they were signaling a message, then left in a hurry.

I quickly picked up the dishes off the table and filled the sink with Jergens dish soap and let them soak. I swept the kitchen floor, emptied the dust pan into the garbage and hung the dust pan back onto the hook in the laundry room. I just finished my chores when I heard Mother's Austin chug up the lane.

I waited at the side door for her. I wanted to catch her mood. She edged the car into the garage, shut off the engine and opened her car door. She looked furious. I wondered if the officers did not keep their promise and told Mother what happened.

She hated me watching her. I turned my head, and I heard her slam the car door.

"Why are you standing there gawking, Maddy? Start my tea."

I needed to get the words out, now or never.

"Something happened today, Mother."

"It can wait for now, Maddy. Tell me after my tea. Put the kettle on, and then unload the groceries from the backseat."

After I put the kettle on, made the tea and unloaded the groceries, I poured a cup for myself as well and then sat down with Mother at the table.

My hands started to tremble as I prepared to tell Mother what happened. I put the teacup down carefully before she noticed my nervousness, but it rattled as I placed it on the saucer.

Mother looked up, her face contorted with anger.

"What now, Maddy! Spit it out!"

Mother listened without comment as I spilled out what happened. I glazed over the details of the rape to spare her. She stared at me coldly until I was finished. She didn't pull me toward her and engulf me in a hug, as I'd hoped she would. She was disengaged as if she were not involved in the story. She showed no emotion.

Mother finished her tea before me. I had to force myself to swallow, so I had a lot left in my cup. Mother wouldn't allow waste.

She picked up her cup, walked over to the kitchen sink and then rinsed the cup out.

Her back was to me when she said, "So, he raped you! I warned you! You've only yourself to blame. Here, make yourself useful and clean up the tea dishes. When you've finished, go up to your room. I don't need to see that sad face. You got what you deserved for not listening to me."

I was shocked at Mother's reaction. I recognized the look on her face. I understood that it wasn't anger or loathing. It was vast indifference. My heart ached. What I sought, what I required, was for Mother to draw me into a hug and hold me tight. But it wasn't going to come about. So, now there was just the two of us, alone in this huge house, one mad and one tainted for life. I walked over to the sink and dumped the tea into it with a splash.

As Mother left the room, she spat over her shoulder.

"And stop sniveling! It won't help anything. You got what you deserved!"

The shrill ring of the telephone shattered the silence just as Mother was heading for her bedroom. I remained washing the dishes, as Mother would want to answer it or not.

Mother let out a deep sigh as she shuffled over to the phone. Her mouth tightened into a thin line.

I heard Mother say in a loud, firm voice, "No, that won't be necessary. No, I won't be pressing charges."

The officer must have protested as Mother started to shout, "This discussion is closed. Don't call again."

I knew I was done for. I feared for Erin. She would not be rescued. Mother did not like any touch of scandal on the family. And I had told. Raymond would harm Erin. That was for sure. I had made a bad mistake.

I had committed the cardinal sin. I interrupted.

"Mom? Erin, what about Erin?"

"Shut up, Maddy! You both deserved what you got!"

Officer Kent must have pressed on.

Mother repeated, "No, I won't discuss this again!" Then, "Erin got herself into that mess. She can get herself out of it!"

My heart sank and hammered erratically against my chest. Mother smashed the phone down with such a force it made me jump in my chair.

Mother stepped toward me then and put her face right up to mine.

"I don't want to hear anymore of this from you, either. I am tired. I am going to bed. No more disturbances, do you understand me?"

I filled the sink with warm sudsy water and began to wash the supper dishes. The hot water relaxed me and allowed the tears to loosen and stream down my face. I had to stop every few minutes to wipe my face and nose. Finally I was finished and was able to go up to bed. I tried hard not to think about the rape. No matter how hard I tried though, I could think of nothing else. I pulled the blankets up to my chin and lay still, but still my skin prickled with nerves.

After several attempts to fall asleep, I finally succumbed to exhaustion. I fell into a light sleep, but flashbacks of the day kept haunting me. I knew I would never see my sister again. Dark smothering grief pulled me down, threatening to drown me in the deep depths of despair. If Raymond killed Erin, I would be responsible for another death.

I awoke from a troubled night the next morning not knowing what to expect from Mother. I walked down the stairs for breakfast with caution, filled to the brim with an intense sense of doom. Mother sat at the kitchen table reading. She did not glance up to acknowledge my presence. She continued to ignore me when I sat down with my coffee and toast. My alarm bells were sounding danger. What was Mother planning? I brought disgrace to her by disobeying her. Would she get rid of me, too? Rather than a sniff of scandal to our family, she would sweep us all away clean.

That whole day was unbearable. Mother had scarcely spoken two words to me since I told her about the rape. She kept me in suspense.

What I remember about that year when Father died, from the funeral right through the eight months to the rape, was the huge empty hole in my heart. I often wondered, *How could this emptiness inside cause me to feel so heavy?*

FIREWEED ISLAND, JUNE 1959

After school let out on a bright warm day in June, a few weeks before high school graduation, my life's journey took another sharp turn onto a dangerous path. The days were hot. "Dog days," mother called them. Our last class of the day was a study period. The class was restless; all our thoughts were on the future. I glanced out to the tarmac parking lot. Mirage-like waves of heat hovered over the surface. A large black fly buzzed loudly around the room, looking for escape from the classroom. Much like the rest of us, I thought. At last the bell rang out, and we made our getaway. I made my way to the bus. My friends were meeting at the dairy for Cokes, but I had to get home. Mother was on her day off. She expected me home.

The closer I got to home, the more nervous I became. I had a strong sense of dread. Something was clearly wrong. I didn't know what to expect from her these days. It was a crapshoot. Her spirits escalated swiftly from cavernous lows to lofty heights, lingered there for a while, then plummeted back down as rapidly as a downhill skier. Once she hit bottom, she lay stranded in the dark depths of despair for days.

I was parched. I longed for a cold glass of lemonade. I quickened my pace. The garage door to our kitchen hallway was ajar. I heard soft music coming from our radio in the kitchen. I slipped in to the kitchen quietly. Mother had her back to me. She was rolling out pastry for butter tarts on a floured board on the kitchen table. Her head was bent over the table, concentrating on her task. Her thick, curly auburn hair was pulled back into a bun.

A loose strand escaped and spiraled down her pale neck. Her thin neck made her seem fragile and vulnerable to me. She wore a light blue dress and a bib apron. Her sleeves were rolled up to her elbows. She was singing along with the radio. This was a good sign. She must be having a good day.

A fresh breeze slipped into our kitchen through the window facing the lake. I went straight to the counter where some butter tarts were cooling. The scent of the warm brown sugar and cinnamon made my mouth water.

I walked over, picked one up and started to munch on it.

"Yummy. Good, Mother!"

She turned to face me. Despite the breeze, Mother had beads of sweat on her brow and above her upper lip.

I was very mistaken about her mood. She growled like an angry dog.

"Sit down. I have something to talk to you about."

Her manner and her tone of voice clanged like a shrill hurricane warning in my head. My high spirits deflated and spiraled to the ground like a helium balloon with the air let out.

I plunked down at the kitchen table with my eyes cast down, waiting for the blow. I heard her soft footsteps approach. I glimpsed up at her. She quickly glanced away. One look at her grim face with her mouth set in a thin line sent my heart galloping. Mother picked up her empty tea cup and set it down again.

I picked up the teapot and poured her tea, waiting for the hit.

She was distracted, nervous.

"What are your plans after graduation?"

I did not pause with my answer as I had already made my decision some time ago. I was prepared for her question.

"I will see if I can work at the bank in town, and I can start paying you room and board. Also, I can save for university."

Mother picked up the teapot in front of her and began to refill her cup.

"I have other plans for you. You will stay at your Aunt Gert's in Vancouver until you get a job. I will give you some money for your room and board until you are able to take care of yourself."

Mother's words took aim at my heart and pierced it. *Why is this happening to me,* I thought *I'm not a bad person, am I? What have I done to her?*

Right at that moment she blew apart any hope that we could ever become close. She smashed to smithereens any thought that I might be able to save enough to enter university next year. I thought perhaps I could help her out, too. She wanted me gone, instead.

Still, I tried to reason with her.

"Mother, no!"

"Save me from your hysterics, Maddy. I have made up my mind!"

The realization that I was being tossed out, the minute, sharp, stinging facts, like sharp rocks I was being stoned with, over and over in those first few minutes, struck my mind. Were all my memories of my family to be left behind here, too? Who will I be without a past? Now, without the possibility of university, who will I be without a future?

Then the sick realization smacked me in the face. This has transpired. A wrecking ball has demolished our family, breaking apart each family member from the foundation of our home, each falling to the earth and disintegrating into dust. Then, just as suddenly, the realization escaped my mind. I couldn't grasp it. It was like some cruel prank.

Now, standing at the kitchen sink, this comprehension levitated above me, hovering like a murky cloud. I comprehended that my life would become one continual horrendous storm. I would be tossed from disaster to disaster. Much later in life, I came to realize that my thoughts could not have been more eerily prophetic.

I got up from my chair quickly to approach her, and I started to speak, "Mom, can't I please stay and help out?"

Mother rose up from her chair in a flash. She thrust me aside as if I were a piece of furniture.

"My job with you is done. I have put up with you long enough. You've been nothing but trouble since the day you were born!"

She left for her bedroom without another word. I put my head down on the kitchen table, devastated. I heard her stomp quickly down the hall, her sharp heels clicking loudly against the floor.

Not long after she left, I heard her dragging something out of her closet. She pulled something behind her as she reentered the kitchen. It was a set of white luggage. I was stunned.

"Take this to your room. Pack all your clothes. I will drive you to the bus depot the weekend after graduation. Someone will drop off your other belongings once you are settled. No need to keep in touch."

She dropped the luggage in front of me and then turned her back on me. She walked down the hall to her room again, closing the door firmly and locking it with a smart snap.

Clutching the kitchen chair beside me to steady myself, I stood staring at the pristine white luggage. All the while the truth raced rat-a-tat through my mind like a steel ball racing down a pinball machine. She wanted me gone. Was I a bad person?

I stumbled over to the kitchen window overlooking the lake. I stood there without moving. I gripped the counter and looked down at the flour dust, the plastic bag of pecans, and the glass container of brown sugar. The sweet aroma of the warm brown sugar and pecans of the butter tarts turned my stomach. The cruel irony of Mother's baking and the reality of her heartlessness staggered me and brought me to my knees.

During the final weeks of school before graduation, I went through the motions, pretending excitement about my future, like my friends, but I was numb inside. I was being discarded by the only person I thought I could depend on.

Graduation was a blur. When my name was announced to receive my diploma, my eyes searched the crowd, hoping to see my mother's face. She was absent. She was serious about tossing me out. I thought she would change her mind, that she was just having a bad day. I was so wrong.

Saturday morning I slept in. I did not hear Mother go to work. I had come right home after the graduation ceremonies. I had nothing to celebrate.

I spent the morning cleaning my room, and then I sped off on my bike to race down the main island road to the highway. I cycled for some time then stopped at a small creek along the highway to eat my cheese sandwich and drink my orange juice from the thermos. I had to keep busy to still my thoughts about the horrible abandonment by my mother. I was fearful of my future now. I didn't know Aunt Gert. She had been shunned from our family some time ago. My mother and her sisters bullied Aunt Gert until she finally divorced Uncle George and left without her children. Why would she send me to someone she not only disapproved of but didn't communicate with? Clearly, Mother put me in the same category as Aunt Gert. I was being excommunicated, shunned.

I decided to make the best of a situation I could not change. I would get a job, do the best I could and become successful. I knew the best revenge was a successful life.

VANCOUVER, JULY 1959

Aunt Gert made me feel very welcome when I arrived in Vancouver. Her apartment was small, too small for me to stay long. I slept on her pullout sofa. I felt obligated to find work right away to help with the expenses. The morning after I arrived, I got up early to look for work.

I was dressed and ready to go out the door when Aunty Gert stopped me.

"Is that what you are wearing?"

"It's not okay?" My heart sank. I had no business clothes. I looked like a ragamuffin in my old dress.

"Wear my new coat over your dress. They won't be interviewing you today, anyway. We will think of something later."

Aunty Gert reached for her new navy blue coat and helped me into it. It hung on me. It was far too big, but it was the only solution.

I walked down one side of Granville Street in the city and entered any business that I thought would hire me and left my name there. I ambled down the street in an unhurried pace. I breathed in the city's hustle and bustle, the blast of horns and the tempest of traffic. I was unfamiliar with the racket. People brushed me aside as they passed. Every block I walked and every refusal of employment made me more determined to succeed. In some ways I felt free.

The mammoth granite bank with the wide steps and large golden door at the end of the last block on Granville Street

74

beckoned. I loved the old grandeur of the establishment.

I walked up the concrete steps to the door and pushed it open with a flourish. I was too desperate for work to be intimidated by the luxurious seating area, the high ceiling and thick, rich carpet.

A tall lady with thick, curly, grey hair approached me at the counter.

"How can I help you?"

"I need work," I said without preamble.

The woman eyed me steadily.

"Just a moment."

I overheard her say to a coworker.

"Come, see this!"

They both advanced toward the counter again.

I introduced myself the way Aunt Gert and I had practiced.

"Hello, I am Maddy Richardson. I am looking for any work that you may have available. I am a high school graduate."

My chest was tight. My breath was weak.

The coworker, a tall, smartly dressed woman in a red suit with black velvet trim, looked at me intently.

"Aren't you a friend of my nephew, Jake?"

I was surprised that she knew of me. I did recall that Jake mentioned that his aunty worked at a bank. I didn't know which one.

"Yes," I replied. My voice came out like a boom. They may give me a chance here, I thought.

"Come in tomorrow at ten o'clock, and we will interview you."

"Thank you," I managed. I was amazed that I was being considered.

Just as I was turning away, I overheard one of them say, "Did you see that coat on her? It is huge on her! She must have borrowed it, poor lamb."

I was elated that I was going to be considered for work but upset that I was being pitied. This was a blow to my pride. It could be a poor start to a new job.

Several weeks later at the bank, I was astonished to see Jake walk in and talk to his aunt. I was with a customer at the teller's cage. He gave me a slight wave when he recognized me. I tilted my head up and smiled. His face lit up like a light bulb, his smile as wide as a mile. It seemed as if no time had passed since we saw each other last.

After my customer had left, Jake walked over.

"Had your coffee break?"

"Actually, no." I was mesmerized by his sudden appearance. I thought I was seeing an apparition.

"I'll check with my supervisor," I said.

"Already have. We can take a half hour if we like."

"I was surprised to hear that Anne is your aunt. I had no idea! It is great to see you!"

Jake and I picked up where we had left off, as if we had never parted. We began to see each other regularly, cautiously at first, as he was wary of my restlessness. It took awhile for him to trust me again.

VANCOUVER, JULY 1959

Several months later, we rented an apartment together. On a weekend that Jake was working on the fishing boats, I was tidying up our small apartment. The phone rang as I was gathering up our laundry to wash.

"Hello?"

"Is this Maddy Richardson?" The voice was professional, with a distinct softness to it.

"Yes, who is this?"

"This is Mission Hospital. Your mother has had a cerebral hemorrhage. I am sorry to say that she isn't doing well."

"I'll be there as soon as I can."

I phoned Jake's boss and relayed the message that I had to leave town immediately, then ran to catch the six p.m. train to Mission.

I cannot recall the journey there. I only remember the urgency I felt to get to Mother as fast as I could. Finally, she would recognize my love for her. I knew she would recover, and we would become close. We could help each other.

I just caught the train in time. Once I disembarked, I hailed a taxi, and I was at the hospital by nine p.m. The light in the hospital lobby was stark against the dark evening outside. My heart was pounding when I asked the receptionist for my mother's room. I hesitated before opening her door. How would I find her? Mother's room was dim. A small reading lamp on the bedside table lit Mother's face. She looked small as a child. My heart pitched. She looked so defenseless. Her eyes were closed. I thought perhaps she was asleep. She started to stir then opened her eyes slowly. She glared up at me. Her lips were drawn into a thin line.

"Maddy, what are you doing here?"

I didn't want to alarm her.

I hesitated, and then said, "The hospital phoned to let me know you were here. I came to see if I could help you until you were on your feet."

"Where is Erin? I want Erin. Ask her to come. You needn't bother to stay," she said.

Shock silenced me, and then a rush of anger pulsed through me like a blender, shaking me to bits. Mother wounded me as she had never wounded me before. Even now, after all these years, I still recoil from the memory.

I telephoned Erin from the bank of telephones in the hospital lobby, and then I returned to Vancouver on the ten p.m. train. I recall very little of the journey home.

Later I would convince myself I'd seen moisture around Mother's eyes, but what struck me then was her abject dispassion. What I remember most was her faraway look. I was starkly reminded of how often in the past she had been distant and cold. There were times when I would search for what I had said or done to upset her. Now, as an adult, I realize that it was naive to believe that I was even partially to blame, but I always would.

Mother died in her sleep that night. She was forty-eight years old. I was seventeen and still a stupid, stupid child. I was rejected by the one person who should have cared for me. That I was unlovable became very clear to me the morning after she passed on.

Grief and all the unresolved issues that Mother and I had led to my meltdown the following week. I packed a few things in Jake's apartment in a daze while he was at sea and left. I removed myself from the one person left in this world I cared about. I couldn't chance being rejected again. It was best to disappear.

I moved back to Aunt Gert's. We soon found her apartment too small for the both of us, so I moved to a basement suite nearby and settled there, aimlessly living day to day. I was adrift like a balloon in the sky. I was anonymous in the big city. I gave no thought to how my actions might have affected Jake. I just felt a compelling need to run. Several months slipped by in a fog that felt both unsettling and unending.

After several months of coasting, I soon became bored and started looking for employment. Eventually luck was with me. I secured a job in a government office, and I settled down.

AUSTRALIA, 2006

Those memories still haunt me after all these years. Tom shut me out just as surely as my mother had forty years ago. I cleaned up the kitchen after yet another fight that began at dinner and continued until Tom played himself out and took himself to his bed. He had an early pickup the next morning. After he left for the bedroom, I made myself an instant coffee and set out for the living room. I switched on the TV, but I could not focus on it. I faced the same sense of abandonment and distance from Tom as I had from Mother after the rape. Tom isolated me. I understood that now. The only friend I had here was Lydia. I met her on one of my walks in the afternoon around the saltwater lake nearby. She lived a few blocks from our place in a cul-de-sac. Her house was not visible from the road. Instinct warned me to keep our friendship a secret from Tom and everyone else.

Tom inspired in me the same phantom guilt that haunted me while I was living with Mother. I hadn't done anything wrong, but I was blamed for someone else's crime, and I had accepted the responsibility. Had someone cut Tom off on the road? Had Paula and he had words? My thoughts scurried in my head like a gerbil on a spinning wheel. I got up and tried to make myself comfortable on the old sofa, enveloping myself in an old afghan. I wrapped it around myself tightly for warmth. I kept my shoes on and wrapped my hand around my house keys in my pocket for a fast escape if necessary. Finally, I drifted off to a light, disturbed sleep, listening for any sign that Tom was stirring and I was in danger.

Tom started to slam about the house at three a.m. He was leaving soon to drive people to the airport. I knew that he was trying to wake me on purpose, not to make amends, but to agitate me. Too exhausted to argue, I feigned sleep until I heard his car drive off. Once he had gone, I slipped into sleep again. I slept soundly and deeply, knowing that I was safe for several hours.

The insistent ring of the telephone drew me out of a subterranean sleep. I drifted up through a wall of water and hurried from the sofa, kicking off the afghan that tangled around my feet. I couldn't imagine who it might be. Tom did not encourage visitors, so I made few friends.

I answered cautiously, not knowing who or what to expect. "Hello?"

"It's me, Holly!

What a relief! It was an old friend from Canada, who knew me well.

"Hi, Holly! What's new? It's so good to hear your voice!"

"I've got exciting news. Ted and I have made travel arrangements to come visit you!"

A feeling of excitement, then simultaneously a sick realization hit me. Holly was very perceptive. She always had the uncanny ability to assess a situation for what it was and to get to the bottom of things quickly. I wasn't prepared to let her know the truth about my marriage. I was so afraid Holly would see my marriage for the sham that it was.

I tried to sound enthusiastic.

"Great! When are you coming, and where are you landing?"

Holly was ecstatic.

"Can you meet us in Cannes? Ted wants to see the reef."

I rallied and answered in what I hoped portrayed some eagerness.

"I'll check with Tom and get back to you, but I am sure we can arrange it."

"I am so excited! I can't wait to see you. I want to know Tom better, too."

"Okay, I am sure we can meet you, but I will phone you as soon as I know to confirm."

How could I confess anything about my situation? It was so

shameful. I couldn't, not now, not when they were coming here expecting a great holiday. They had been saving up for months. I could not spoil their trip.

I hung up and then went to make coffee to wake up. The night frets still lingered. I hoped strong coffee would give me a quick jolt to pull me out of the fog I was in. I went into the bedroom and scrambled with my hands in my dresser drawer to find the socks where I had hidden two cigarettes I had stolen from Tom last night.

I was so afraid Holly would see the marriage for what it was, see everything: my disappointed eyes when Tom merely shrugged to answer a question from me, or my irritation when he got up from the table and left the room while I was still eating, and most of all, the cold, disinterested, and condescending way Tom spoke down to me.

Deeply disturbed, I walked to the bathroom and glanced into the mirror to see a gaunt face. I had lost so much weight. I looked like a Biafra refugee. When had I started letting myself go? I needed a haircut and an eyebrow wax. My wrinkles were deeper than ever. Dark circles framed my eyes. Holly would notice the change in me immediately.

***

The eve of Holly's arrival came quickly. Tom and I were going to be picked up by bus to take us to the airport in Sydney. From there we would fly to Cannes to meet Holly and Ted.

I had packed my suitcase that afternoon and prepared Tom's clothes for him to pack in his own suitcase. When he arrived home from work, he entered the house in good spirits. He headed straight for the fridge and pulled out a cold can of beer.

"I'm going down for a quick beer at the old guys' house. I won't be long. You didn't pack my suitcase, did you? You're hopeless at it."

I stopped myself from responding. This was not the time to argue. I would need to be very careful not to set him off this evening, especially if he had been drinking.

He let the screen door slam behind him as he left.

I put our dinner on hold. I could hear the men's voices sounding more and more rambunctious, their voices and laughter loud and coarse.

I sensed trouble ahead. Sure enough, Tom returned home a few minutes later, empty beer can in hand. The look in his eyes was all too familiar. He looked right through me.

He marched to the fridge, tossed the empty can into a cardboard box beside the fridge and pulled out another beer.

"I'll be back in a few minutes. I told the guys that if they managed their money like me, they could travel too."

I cringed with embarrassment at his words. Tom was very egotistical. It sounded as if he were lecturing them again. He would be the laughing stock in the entire leisure village. The 'old guys' were all retired professionals. There would be a great discussion about him after he left, I was sure.

Tom returned a half an hour later for yet another beer. He swept open the screen door with a strange looking flourish then released it, causing a loud crash behind him. The sound reverberated in the silence of the room. He gave me a sideways sneer as he straggled in. He was clearly inebriated. My heart sank as I witnessed him stagger over to the fridge for another beer.

Could he see my dread? See my debility? I must hide my alarm. If he perceived I was frightened, he would pounce on it, like a wolf smelling blood.

He was attempting to hide his unsteadiness without success.

"What are you looking at?"

I dodged the question.

"Are you hungry? Your clothes are all ready to pack."

Tom snatched another beer from the fridge and started back to the door.

He tossed the words at me over his shoulder.

"I'll eat when I am ready, and I will pack when I am ready, bitch!"

In disgust, I tossed the cold chops and potatoes in the trash. He wouldn't want to eat when he got home. I quickly cleaned up the kitchen and made myself a fresh pot of coffee.

I could hear the boys becoming more and more rowdy and loud down the street. I heard Tom's raspy voice rise above the others. This alarmed me. Tom was always abusive when he was drunk, without fail.

The airport bus was booked for 2:30 a.m. He would either fall asleep when he straggled in or become violent, fifty/fifty. It was too late to change plans with Holly. They were already on their flight. I could only hope for the best, that I could avoid him, and that he might fall asleep immediately and get a few hours sleep before the bus arrived.

I heard Tom's raspy shout saying goodbye to the men down the street, heard Tom shuffling up the stairs onto our verandah, heard the door slam shut. I was too aware of what that meant.

I had to put some distance between us. I needed to get out of his reach. I turned my back to him and entered the tiny kitchen to put my coffee cup in the sink. I was trying to buy time. I did not trust myself to look at him. He might see my fear or perceive some weakness in me to seize upon.

Spittle shot out of the corner of his mouth as he barked at me, "Where do you think you're going?"

My stomach coiled into a tight knot. I couldn't escape, but I continued to walk away from him. He caught up to me. He stretched his right arm around my neck and squeezed, then pulled my head back toward him in a fierce grip. I tasted the salty sweat where his arm pressed against my mouth. My blouse caught under his arm and twisted tightly around my neck, throttling me.

My throat constricted painfully. Just when the pain became unbearable, he released me and hurled me forward. I stumbled but managed to stay upright. I whipped around to face him. I understood at that split second that we might have our worst fight the night before we were to meet Holly and Ted.

I needed to de-escalate Tom's fury, and fast. I stepped away quietly and made my way to the bedroom.

"I'm going to bed, Tom. I left your suitcase and clothes ready for you to pack on the dining room table."

His voice, harsh and cutting, said, "I don't know why I married you! You are useless for anything! Get out!"

I was stunned. This was worse than anything I could have imagined.

Tom lunged toward my back, again. He grabbed my arm, squeezing it like a vise, and yanked me around like a whip. He shoved me backwards toward the front screen door. Reaching the door, he thrust my body brutally toward the wall beside it. The back of my head smashed against the door frame. My head snapped. He held me there with one strong arm and stretched to open the screen door. He threw me out as if I were an errant dog. My back hit the verandah post. There was a sudden crack that might have been my arm, or it might have been the sound of my head again hitting the verandah post.

I slid down to the verandah floor and lay still against the post. Everything inside of me felt broken.

I struggled to stay alert. If I passed out now, he would finish me off. I screamed for help. It was my only chance. I saw a curtain flutter and some light from my neighbor Agnes' house. Agnes had pulled her kitchen curtain aside and was peering out. Then she shut the curtain quickly and shut her light out as well. My last chance for help was gone.

I closed my eyes, swimming in agony. Then I heard Tom's footsteps approaching. Surely not, what more harm can he do? He stood over me. I was too weak to get out of his way.

"Shut up! What will the neighbors think?"

He looked at me with revulsion then he kicked my legs, kicked my thighs, kicked my stomach over and over and over. I didn't think I would survive the blows. Once he had spent his anger, he returned to the house, leaving me in a heap. I crawled over to the bench on the verandah. I curled up in a ball, a cowering animal, crying helplessly to the heavens. Bile gushed up to my mouth the way it does before you vomit. I swallowed it down, too weak and too sore to move. I fell under a thin layer of semi-conscious sleep.

I was awakened what seemed seconds later by a blinding flashlight shining into my face. It was Tom. I was stiff from the cold. My bruises were sore. I heard the airport bus rumble up the road before I saw the headlights drawing near.

Tom pulled me up roughly.

"Get a move on. The bus is here!"

I limped to the bathroom. With slow deliberate steps, I went to the sink and doused my face with warm water. I pulled a sweater from the hook by the door, picked up my suitcase and followed Tom to the waiting vehicle.

***

I was excited to see my old friend again, but anxiety continually ragged jarringly around my head. Would she notice Tom's abuse? Had I covered my bruises sufficiently? Holly was very intuitive. She always sensed when I was being evasive. I had never had a reason to be anything but honest with her in all the years we were friends, and I never had to hide anything from her in the past.

The minute I saw her I melted. I felt safe. I didn't want to spoil their trip, so I feigned any trepidation and plunged into a holiday mode. Tom would be on his best behavior, surely.

We sped off to Point Douglas and the white sandy beaches. Trendy restaurants and boutiques beckoned us down a lovely shaded street. Tourists mobbed the outdoor restaurant patios, making a colorful display of movement and gaiety. Laughter rang out from the tables and spilled over the cobbled streets.

When we were all ready for lunch, and we were walking down the sidewalk, Holly exclaimed in glee, "Oh, let's go there!"

Tom pulled me away.

"That's too pricey! We'll find something else."

He scurried ahead in front of us, hurrying us all along, clucking at us like a mother hen.

"There's a pub. We will go there!"

I was acutely embarrassed. For dinner, we ended up at a family restaurant that served roast beef with white sauce over steamed vegetables, hardly the menu we, other than Tom, were craving that hot day. Ted, Holly and I were sipping our wine and enjoying our conversation before we ordered. Tom again hurried us along. We needed to eat and travel a further one hundred miles before we stopped for dinner.

86

What should have been a wonderful, memorable, carefree holiday turned out to be a nightmare. I tried to approach Holly about my situation many times. It was the constant menace of Tom's sudden appearance when the two of us were alone for a moment or two that made me nervous and too afraid to reveal anything.

LIGHTNING RIDGE, AUSTRALIA, 2006

Four weeks into our trip we headed for the opal mining fields and the town of Lightning Ridge. Holly wanted to purchase an opal ring from the large opal store in the mining town. I had been there last year with Tom. I was enchanted with the town and its unique surroundings and cast of colorful characters.

We were silent for miles. Tom had the air conditioner on full blast. We were chilled to the bone.

"Tom, can we turn the air conditioner down a little?"

"No, it is hot as hell out there!"

"Please, we are all cold!"

"You're not listening! I said no!"

Holly whispered to me, "Don't we get a vote?"

Tom overheard, "Did you say something, Holly?"

"Nothing important, Tom."

Holly looked at me oddly. Did she think it unlike me to succumb so easily? This was so out of character for me. There would be hell to pay after Holly and Ted left for their cabin after dinner. My spirits sank to rock bottom and lodged there for the entire day. The atmosphere inside the car became tense.

As we drove through miles and miles of barren land, the silence grew to be unnerving. I reminded myself that I was not responsible for Tom's behavior, but I knew Holly would think I was an idiot for marrying him. My pride was sinking along with my spirits. I decided that I could not hide my situation any longer.

It was stark and ugly. Worse, it was now exposed to Holly

and Ted. Perhaps they would understand and help me get back to Canada.

All at once, Holly sat straight up from her slumped position.

"Look! Over there!" She was pointing to the left. An eagle had scooped up a baby pig at least its own size. Tom brought the car to a halt. We watched in awe as the eagle soared almost straight up in the sky, like a plane taking off from a runway, then dropped the pig on the rocks below. He circled only once, and then he flew down in a flash and scooped up the injured pig. Again he dropped the pig on the rocks. This time, he circled twice, flew down close to the pig as if to assess the damage, soared up in the sky again, and swooped down and picked up the pig for the third time, this time flying off with it.

Tom turned on the ignition again without a word, and we sped off, silent again, amazed at what we had just witnessed. A profound sadness welled up inside me. I could not help but think that a difference in Tom's attitude would make our trip so much more enjoyable. I reminded myself: *what could have been, Maddy, not what is.*

Ahead of us in the far distance we saw the town of Lightning Ridge. We pulled the car to the side of the road to peer at the sight. We stumbled out of the car, grateful to escape from the icy air inside the car. It was like stepping inside a sauna. The heat was overpowering. I gazed down the street. The heat rose up from the gravel. The town shimmered in the heat like a mirage. I felt if I were to walk toward the town that it would disappear.

A road sign advertised the Bore Hole Pool that I so enjoyed the last time I was here. The pool was a warm seventy-eight degrees and rose from an underground well. I felt my heart quicken. I looked forward to a second visit there.

We found our motel, and we separated from Ted and Holly to put our luggage into our respective rooms. We agreed to meet at the pub up the street for lunch in a half hour.

As soon as Holly and Ted left, Tom started in on me.

"Why did you complain about the air conditioning? It made me look incompetent!"

"Incompetent? What does the temperature of the air conditioning have to do with incompetency?"

I became conscious that Tom was spoiling for a fight. I knew I should keep my mouth shut. His narcissistic air and sense of self-importance stunned me. I answered in reflex without thought.

I feared that he would hit me. If they saw any more marks and bruises, then I could no longer pretend our marriage was anything but a sham. I needed to keep my cool.

He only issued me a warning.

"I'll let this go, this time."

I knew at that moment that I would be safe while I was with my friends. Tom had too much pride to allow them to see any physical abuse, at least. I assumed that he was not aware of the daily psychological abuse he subjected me to that was very visible to anyone around us.

I quickly unpacked our suitcases while Tom paced the floor.

"Hurry up! Go get them."

"Who? Ted and Holly?"

"Who else? Just do as I say, Maddy."

I was hesitant to rush them but had no choice in the matter. If I delayed going over to their cabin, it would annoy Tom further, and he would sulk throughout our entire lunch. I decided to walk over to their cabin. It was the lesser of two evils. Once I got there, I found their front door ajar. As I lifted my hand to knock, I saw Holly with a large glass of smooth white liquid in her hand. It was vodka. She looked startled to see me and then turned sharply away. She then walked rapidly into the kitchen. I witnessed her furtively place the full glass into a kitchen cabinet.

"Holly, for goodness sake, have your drink. I don't blame you. Tom would drive anyone to drink!"

"I will, then. Want one?"

"No, thanks. Tom wants to get going. I will meet you at the restaurant. You know how to get there?"

"Yes, we won't be long."

As I raced back to our cabin, Tom was standing at the stoop, waiting, edgy and irritable.

"Hurry along!"

I scurried into the cabin to grab my purse, and when I came out Tom was walking rapidly up the road toward the restaurant. I scampered behind him to catch up. In my haste, I brushed past a young man strolling down the path, knocking his newspaper out of his hand.

"Whoa, what's the rush?"

"Sorry!"

He bent down to retrieve his paper and then looked ahead to where Tom was standing with his hand on his hips, scowling, watching in disgust.

"What's his problem? Are you in some sort of trouble here?"

"No, it's okay, thanks."

I thought, *This is not a good way to start a lunch. Holly is drinking, and Tom is annoyed, no, is in more like a rage. I am sunk! I am so sick of the embarrassment and fear. I'm going to have to ask Holly for help.*

Tom turned and continued to stride down the sidewalk until he reached the restaurant. I finally caught up behind him just as he approached the door. He pulled it open angrily then stepped in, letting the door slam behind him right in my face.

I waited a moment. I felt too embarrassed to step in right behind him. I had no choice. We were meeting Holly and Ted there. I opened the door and held my head up, trying to look nonchalant. Tom was chatting up the hostess, laughing, using his charm. *He's a magician,* I thought as I watched him. *He can pull up charm from an empty hat.*

I waited until Tom was seated before I walked over to sit down at his table.

"What's keeping your friends, then, eh?"

"They'll be along. What looks good on the menu?"

"Nothing. We should have gone to the pub. It's cheaper."

Just then, Holly and Ted entered the restaurant, saving me from having to reply to Tom's complaint. I raised my hand to beckon them. Holly's stride was a little off. She almost tripped as she stepped aside from a passing waiter. She slid into the seat and reached for the menu.

"What are you having, Maddy?"

"The soup and Reuben sandwich."

Tom cut in sharply.

"She should have had the prawns. She could have made a Reuben sandwich at the motel kitchenette if that was all she was having."

Holly's face showed her contempt.

"Do you feel like having the prawns, Maddy?"

I needed to save the day. I couldn't risk an argument, so I smiled as I made my reply.

"Both look appealing."

Thankfully, Ted sensed my discomfort, so he began a conversation right away with Tom about the history of Lightning Ridge and the miners that lived here.

I looked around. The restaurant was buzzing. Most of the customers were tourists, but a few were locals. They all wandered in, reached over the counter, picked up a cup, then helped themselves to coffee from the big urn. Holly was distracted and unfocused. I decided against engaging her in conversation. Black and white photos of Lightning Ridge miners and the town from its beginning until the present graced the walls. A huge mining pick hung above the photos.

I was surprised to see the man I had brushed up against on the sidewalk earlier enter the restaurant. He nodded to the hostess, who was seating patrons, then walked over to an empty table next to us.

The waitress rushed over as soon as he was seated to pour him coffee.

"The usual?"

His smile was bright and warm.

"Yes, and I will have the special, please."

He glanced across the aisle to our table and caught my eye. He held his gaze on me for a moment then scanned his eyes over our table. His eyes stopped at Tom and scrutinized him for a split second. This made me nervous. I hoped Tom didn't notice. I turned my eyes away and focused on Ted's conversation with the manager of the restaurant about the history of Lightning Ridge.

At last, our lunch arrived. My plate was overflowing with hot, spicy chips. The sandwich was three-tiered, chock-full of meat and oozing with Dijon mustard and sauerkraut. The musty smell of sauerkraut mingled with the mustard produced a mouth-watering aroma. All conversation stopped as we dug in to our lunch.

I was halfway finished with my meal. Ted was savoring the last few chips on his plate and enjoying his cold beer when Tom quickly got up from the table.

"Ready?"

He did this to me all the time, but in front of company? I was mortified.

Collectively, wordlessly, we all decided to give in to Tom's impatience and leave. We paid our bill and walked back to our cabins. Holly was walking a little unsteadily, but she seemed to become more lucid as time wore on. I breathed a sigh of relief.

We all walked toward the car to take us to the opal mine fields when Holly said, "I need to get my straw hat. I'll burn up otherwise."

I said quickly, before Tom could put his word in, "Okay, hurry!"

The rest of us settled into the car. Tom started the engine and pulled over in front of Holly's and Ted's cabin. We waited for a few minutes. Holly was not coming out.

I needed to subdue Tom's impatience.

"I'll get her. She probably can't find it."

When I pushed open the front door of their cabin, I observed Holly putting a glass in the sink. I couldn't chance a confrontation now. I had no choice but to ignore it.

"Holly, hurry up!"

She slipped the vodka bottle into the cupboard, turned and staggered toward me from one side to another like someone on a boat on a high, tumultuous sea. My heart dropped. *Oh, Holly, why?*

I escorted her to the car as quickly as I could manage and then I helped her into the car. The mine was only a short distance. I hoped she could remain awake. I got into the seat on the other side of her and glanced over. She had dropped her head down to her knees. I reached over and gently pulled her head up and attempted to secure her seat belt. She swayed back and forth. It was an impossible task without help. Should I risk asking Ted to help, making Tom aware of the situation? No, I would hope that Tom would drive carefully, and we wouldn't run into highway patrol.

Conversation did not get off the ground while we were driving toward the fields. Holly fell fast asleep. It wasn't long before we saw approaching signs directing us to the opal mines. We soon turned into a rough, gravel road. The scene before us was breathtaking. I had been here a few years before, but the magic of the place returned to me full blast.

I glanced over to Holly. "Holly! Wake up!"

Ted turned his head over his shoulder in the front seat.

"Leave her. She didn't sleep last night."

We locked up the car, leaving the car windows open for Holly, then started our way down the main road to look at the mines. Signs made out of old particleboard, car doors from some nearby car cemetery or paper stapled to fences had claim numbers on them. All signs warned us to keep out. The miners' dwellings were made of particleboard with corrugated iron roofs. They were flimsy shacks. Scrubby trees did little to ease the heat. The air was dense. Breathing was like inhaling cotton candy. Time stood still here. As I passed the dwellings, I could not help but think, *They must hate the tourists gawking at them; I would.*

Soon we were overcome with the heat and dust. We agreed to return to the car and drive to the Opal Shop in town. When we returned, Holly was still fast asleep, lightly snoring. Once I was seated beside her again, I shook her awake.

"Holly, we are going to the shop. It will be cool in there. C'mon, kiddo!"

She gave me one of her small smiles and said, "Sorry, I didn't sleep last night." She sat up, straightened her clothing and became somewhat coherent.

Much as I would have liked to argue the point for her sake, I had no choice but to let it go. I so much wanted to get to the bottom of her drinking. Now was not the time.

The Opal Shop was like a cave, cool and inviting. Rows upon rows of black opals and opal gemstones in deep blues and greens sparkled in glass cases the entire length of the store. There were several tourists browsing the aisles. Ted and Holly approached the man behind the counter. Soon he was pulling out several rings for Holly to try on. It appeared to me that Holly had resurfaced from her alcoholic stupor. My tension eased a little.

Tom was seated by the door, engrossed in reading a brochure on the history of Lightning Ridge. I chuckled to myself. *He'll lecture us on its contents later, I bet!*

I sensed a soft stirring behind me, much like a person might discern a small bird rustling in a bush when one walks in the woods. Strangely, this did not alarm me. I felt no danger. Curious, I turned and faced a large man with a round face and a warm smile. An aura of peace and contentment surrounded him.

His voice was as soothing as a warm bath.

"I am the owner of this store. I was a Franciscan monk for many years. My wife and I bought this establishment a number of years ago. That is my wife, over there, talking to your friends."

I glanced over and saw a lovely, sophisticated looking woman. She was attentive while talking to Ted and Holly.

"They are friends of mine visiting me from Canada."

He turned his head in Tom's direction.

He gave Tom a fleeting look then spoke softly, with conviction, "You need to get away from that man."

I shivered. How did he assess my situation so correctly, so quickly? It was uncanny but somehow believable to me. My trust in the man was instantaneous and unquestionable.

He went on, "Everyone who lives here has a story. We would welcome you. My wife and I would help you settle. My wife would enjoy your company. We have a small airport nearby. We fly away to the city quite frequently to attend an opera, or a play, or just shop."

I was about to reply when Tom stirred, put the brochure down and approached us.

The owner slipped a business card into my pocket then turned away.

The whole incident was surreal. Instinct begged me to keep this to myself, much as I kept my friendship with Lydia a secret.

Tom went to great lengths to stop Holly and me from having any time alone. I may as well have been attached to him with handcuffs. We travelled for miles across Australia, stopping only for a quick bite to eat, then back into the hot vehicle and miles and miles of travel. Seldom did we stop to take a break. The whole holiday was like a marathon, zooming here and there and not taking in the beauty and culture of Australia. I was disappointed for my friends.

I never would have believed that I had so much furtiveness in me, or that I could disassemble so well. I had to compose my face continually to appear serene. Often I wondered if they suspected anything throughout the trip. Seeing Holly had done me a world of good. We had years of shared history. Observing the tenderness and respect she and Ted had together woke me up. It provided the window through which I was able to see things differently, how a good marriage should be.

We dropped them off at their hotel in Sydney a few days earlier than we had originally planned. Ted shook hands with Tom and gave me a big hug.

Holly recoiled from Tom when he approached her.

"The trip has been very interesting, Tom."

I knew with certainty then that I hadn't fooled Holly a bit, but she honored my privacy. This hurt me more than anything, as I felt like I betrayed our friendship by not telling her the truth about my marriage to Tom.

HOME IN AUSTRALIA, 2006

After Holly and Ted's departure for Canada, Tom and I quickly resumed our normal lives. An ugly pattern emerged at home. Tom went to his den as soon as he came home from work, irritable, moody, quick to anger. It was evident to me that Tom was hiding something. He would secrete himself in his den and talk in low, urgent tones to someone on the phone. He also quickly ran to the phone to pick it up before I could reach it should he be away from the den and the door open. On a few occasions, behind the closed door, I heard Tom's voice rise in anger, but the conversation did not make sense to me. I assumed he was talking to Paula.

One evening in September, when Tom had just sat down to our evening meal, the phone rang in his den. He quickly left the table and ran down to answer it. The den door shut behind him. I was curious. These furtive conversations had been going on too long. What was he hiding?

I quietly crept down the hallway to the doorway. I put my ear to the door. I couldn't hear what Tom was saying. He was speaking in such a low pitch. I heard the sharp click of his letter cabinet open, heard paper rustle, and then heard a sharp screech as he closed the metal cabinet. The wheels of his office chair squealed against the wooden floor.

An eerie quiet ensued. Intuition told me he was aware I was behind the door. My heart played a drum roll against my chest. I lifted my head away from the door and knocked quickly.

"Tom, do you want your tea?"

I tried the door. It wasn't locked. I opened it a crack and peered in.

"Tom, do you want me to bring in your tea?"

He hastily closed a file on his desk then hung up the phone swiftly. He must have left the party on the other end of the phone hanging. He swung his chair around to face me, his face a guilty scowl.

"What are you looking at?"

I went for broke.

"You were talking to Paula?"

"It's none of your business whom I am talking to!"

He opened the door wide and brushed past me down the hall to the dining room table. He sat down, waiting for me to serve him.

Our meal was silent. He was wholly absorbed in his precise eating ritual, never lifting his eyes from his plate. Acrid venom slowed my heart. At that moment, I detested him, detested the situation I was in, detested myself.

After he wolfed down his dinner, he shoved his plate aside and rose from the table.

"I am going out for a while. Don't wait up."

I moved my plate to the left.

"Sit down, Tom. We need to talk."

He walked to the hallway and picked his jacket off the hall rack.

"No, we don't have to talk. You have nothing to say that matters to me!" He shrugged into his jacket and went to the door.

At that moment, I lost it. I picked up his dinner plate and threw it like a Frisbee. It smashed against the wall, then exploded and fell to the floor in pieces.

Before Tom could fathom this, I pitched his water toward the wall. The glass bounced and shattered with such force that the glass broke like little pieces of confetti across the room. The light twinkle of the broken glass and the tiny sparkles descending gracefully to the floor.

Tom swiftly turned around to face me. Then he lunged. I turned quickly, barely escaping his grasp. I darted to the china cabinet. I yanked open the glass doors. With one sweep of my hands, I flung all the glassware and china on the bottom shelf to the floor, letting it smash where it may.

Tom charged at me. He pounded his large fists hard on my back with such force it knocked my head against the cabinet's glass door. The glass cracked then broke. The shards flew, shredding my cheeks.

I turned to face Tom. My face must have looked like raw meat. He stood stark still. He gaped at me for a moment, and then he turned his back and walked out the door. I went into the bathroom to administer to my wounds. The lesions were ugly but superficial.

I must leave him, no matter the danger. I was painfully aware that most murders occurred after the woman left her abuser. At least if he should find me after I left, the result would be quick, swifter than the pain I now anticipated and received daily.

I called a taxi and went to the local hospital. The wait was eternal. Every passing minute I was there made it more improbable that I could leave that night. He could return home at any time. I felt all eyes were on me. I looked a fright.

Finally, the nurse in emergency called my name. She led me to a curtained enclosure and inspected my wounds. I evaded her many questions and avoided her eyes, so full of pity. After she cleaned up my wounds, she asked me to wait for the social worker. As soon as she left the room, I slipped out quietly. There was no use in charging Tom with assault. He would disregard the order, and then I would be in worse jeopardy.

When I returned home the house was dark. I entered cautiously, saw no shadows to indicate that he was hiding. He might have followed me to the hospital and assumed that I charged him with assault. I stepped inside like a cat burglar. The air was still. I could not feel his presence. I staggered to the bathroom, feeling dizzy from the painkillers and aftershock.

I hit the light switch. My eyes stung. I shut them away from the light's strong glare for a moment. A screaming headache started at the base of my neck and coursed up to my temples.

I looked up and stared at myself in the mirror. I was a wreck, hideous. I was beginning to rebel against Tom's control. I couldn't stop myself. If I continued this rebellion, I would end up dead. He would end up in jail.

I pulled a blanket out of the linen closet and shambled to the sofa. I needed to be ready for anything. I kept my shoes on, kept my keys in my pocket, ready to run. I wrapped the blanket tightly around me. I was bitterly cold. I began to shake uncontrollably.

I wrapped my hands around the keys in my pocket and slid into a light sleep, my ears alert for the sound of Tom's car.

It wasn't long before the headlights of Tom's car swept across the ceiling. I heard the low growl of his engine as he glided into the garage. I heard the soft purr of the Mercedes motor idling. Then the engine stopped. He slammed the car door shut. His footsteps approached the garage door into our kitchen. He flew the door open with a thump.

I feigned sleep. It was my only chance. Tom brushed past me. He walked directly to the bedroom. He did not come near me. I held my breath, waiting to see what he would do. He fell into the bed, not changing into his pajamas. He pulled the covers up to his ears. He must be inebriated. I prayed that he was drunk enough to sleep for a few hours so I could get some rest. I forced myself to stay awake until I could hear his loud snore. Finally, overwhelming exhaustion overcame me. I was swept like a tide into deep sleep.

The next morning Tom stirred early. I heard him quietly prepare for work.

I closed my eyes and tried to slow my breathing. He tiptoed around, trying not to disturb me. This was unusual. I waited for him to leave, to leave me alone so I could plan an escape.

As he was leaving, he said softly, "Go into our bed, lovey. I won't be home till late." This was disturbing. Why was he speaking so kindly? I didn't know whether to believe him. Was he trying to make me feel safe and therefore unalert? Will he come back with a weapon, a knife, or a gun?

As soon as his car turned into the main road I took action. Still aching and sore, it took me three tries to get up from the old sofa.

My back throbbed with agonizing pain. I hobbled to the bathroom. Tom's scent still lingered there. A strong sulphur odor came from the shower. The mirror was still fogged up. His dirty clothes lay on the floor not a foot from the laundry basket. I bent to pick them up, hugely resentful of having to do this chore while he was so sadistic to me. I hit the ceiling fan switch. It choked and wheezed like an old man. It started to whir and squeal loudly. I needed to hear every sound. I quickly turned it off.

I felt sticky, damp with fear and exhaustion. I was ripe with perspiration, but I could not chance a shower in case he returned. I could not be trapped there. I peed quickly and then washed my arms and neck with lemon-scented soap and a facecloth, avoiding the stinging scrapes on my face.

My head was mush. I walked cautiously into the kitchen to make myself an instant coffee. I must remain alert.

Tom did not return until late that evening. Every passing moment he was late caused me anxiety. When he did finally arrive, he headed straight for the den. I had made dinner at the usual time, but when he didn't arrive home, I put it in on a plate in the microwave.

I spoke to his back.

"Dinner, Tom?"

He walked on, not slowing his pace.

"Not hungry."

He opened the den door and shut it firmly behind him. I heard the lock on the door snap sharply into place. Not long after he entered the den, his phone rang. I heard Tom's excited voice but could not make out his words.

Soon after the phone call I heard him open the door and walk down the hall quietly. He hurriedly pulled his jacket off the rack then pushed the door open to the garage.

I called out.

"Are you going out again?"

"What does it look like to you?" he growled.

I needed to know if I would have time to spend with Lydia to plan my escape.

"When will you be back?"

When he didn't respond I became nervous. I was afraid to leave the house for even an hour. I was trapped.

I paced about the house all that week like a caged animal. I began to talk to myself. It was just like this in the old days when I needed approval from Mother to do something, and I had to plan my approach.

I sat down at the coffee table and forced myself to make a plan of escape. I was so weary and worn down I was beginning not to care. I had to fight to keep up my resolve to leave, fight to gain the will to live.

In the late afternoon on the Friday of that week, Tom's telephone rang. I rushed to the den to answer it. I picked the receiver up and held it to my ear.

"Hello?" There was a second of dead air, then another. I strained to hear. Then I heard a breath.

I brought up a stream of air from my lungs.

"Who is this?"

I struggled to hear some background noise. I heard muffled voices, like they were in a bar. I then heard a murmur at the end of the line. Whoever it was quickly hung up.

Was it Tom, checking up on me?

Goose bumps invaded my arms and legs, causing me to shiver in the afternoon heat. Angst-ridden, I needed to get away, fast. I placed my cup in the kitchen sink, pulled on my sneakers, and left for my friend Lydia's house up the road. I believed that if anyone could come up with a plan of escape, it would be Lydia.

I walked very fast up to Lydia's house. I mounted the steps to her porch. Wind chimes tinkled, and a cat napped on a wicker basket on the verandah. As I approached the door, I could hear Lydia's water spaniels barking excitedly. They scrambled around her feet as she opened the door.

She stared at me for a moment.

"My God, what happened to you?"

Lydia's sympathy was too much for me to handle. I melted

into a puddle of tears. She steered me up to the kitchen, and we sat down at her table.

Lydia listened quietly without interruption. When I finished my story, she hugged me fiercely for a few minutes. We sat at the table until my sobs subsided. Then Lydia made me a cup of tea and put a small measure of whiskey in it. A radio was playing softly in the background. One of Lydia's water spaniels ambled over to my feet and plopped down. A cockatoo sat on an electrical wire nearby, screeching and making a big fuss. It was astounding to me that the world was still spinning, and life was going on while my life had halted into hell.

Lydia finally spoke.

"We need to make a plan." I knew without question that I needed to leave. It was now or never. If I didn't leave now, the moment would pass. I would have no future. Worse, I might be killed. We decided that I would have to return to my home until concrete plans could be made.

I felt a bubble of hope as I walked home. I began a mantra: "I can do this. I can do this."

Suddenly the fog in my brain lifted. I viewed my relationship with Tom in its entirety. For today, at least, I was through with this way of life, with this small cabin, this slice of my life, this whole mess. I was not optimistic. I was not enraged. I was simply finished. I was finished with trying to patch up what could not be mended.

AUSTRALIA,
FEBRUARY 2006

There was a family reunion planned in two weeks. I planned to leave after that. The day of the reunion dawned bright and sunny. It was to be held in a picnic area in the next town. I hadn't met many of Tom's family. He kept me isolated from them. Also, I suspected that he did not get along with many of them. Tom and I entered the park to find the family gathered under large eucalyptus trees. Once we got near, Tom left my side and walked over to a young man standing under the shade of a large tree. He was wearing jeans and a soft blue tee shirt. I stood where I was, watching them. Tom was wearing his awful, stained nylon windbreaker, zipped up to his chin, listening to the young man talking. Tom held his nose haughty in the air as if he smelled something bad.

Tom reached over and pulled a beer from an old laundry tub filled with ice, then began a conversation with the young man. The young man laughed softly at something Tom said and punched him lightly on the arm. I began to feel awkward in the crowd. Not one person came to introduce him or herself to me. Tom did not bother to introduce me to anyone there, so I found myself wandering on the outskirts of the cluster of Tom's relatives. They were seated on blankets under the trees in the park, talking quietly. I walked over to the concrete building that housed the washrooms. I eyed a picnic table and bench behind the building. I walked over to it and sat down. I was out of sight there. I lit up a cigarette and dragged in deeply, trying desperately to remain calm. All the relatives knew who I was, so how would it sound to say, "Hi, I am

Maddy, Tom's wife." I had my back turned away from the park and contemplated how I was to manage this dilemma. I heard a rustle of leaves behind me, so I turned around. It was someone I had not met, but clearly he belonged to the family.

He spoke softly.

"I have known men like Tom before, nice enough when it suits them, but they have no business getting married."

The tenor of his voice calmed me.

"You know Tom well?"

"I have known Tom all my life. I saw how he treated his first wife, Irene. There wasn't a dinner party or a family get-together where he didn't do something to embarrass her. He has a cruel streak in him."

Something loosened inside me then. Finally, someone spoke the truth. It wasn't just me that Tom was mean to. I had seen Tom's cruelty with my own eyes, but I needed to hear it from someone else to fully understand that I wasn't at fault for his temper.

The relief I felt must have shown on my face. He continued to speak in a soft, soothing voice.

"Truth be told, he is a little frightening. People think he's a loose cannon, if you know what I mean. Men like him, they think they own their wives. He thinks his wife is an extension of himself."

"Thank you for telling me. I needed to hear it."

"You didn't hear it from me, understand? I don't need any trouble. I have a family to think of."

"I won't say a word. I promise."

He nodded his head and left. Then he walked away quickly around the back of the building so he would not be noticed. He went to his car and extracted a blanket from the boot of his car and then got lost among the throng of relatives.

Reluctantly, I got up to return to the picnic. Tom would be angry if I did not make some effort to join in. I walked around the building. I started to enter the crowd. I noticed that a photographer was there arranging and rearranging the relatives for a photograph. I slowed my pace, thinking I was probably not to be included in the family portrait. Out of nowhere Tom came barreling down toward me, his arms fiercely waving at me to come over to where the family was gathered.

He raged like a bull.

"Get over here! They're taking a family portrait!"

He grabbed my arm roughly and hurled me forward. My foot tripped on a small twig on the ground, and I fell unceremoniously to my knees. He walked away towards the family assembling for the photo, leaving me on the ground.

He growled, speaking over his shoulder.

"Get up. You're an embarrassment."

As I pulled myself up, I noticed the relatives dart a look at me then quickly glance away. They dismissed the incident as if nothing had happened. Clearly, they were afraid of repercussions from Tom should they come to my aid.

I got up, brushed myself off, then walked over to the photographer. Once there, he positioned me in the photo lineup. I looked straight ahead, too embarrassed to lock eyes with any of the family. I knew I didn't belong there. They didn't know me at all.

I was quiet and kept to myself for the rest of the long afternoon. Tom attempted to approach me on several occasions. He was trying to make people believe we were a loving couple. His pride was his biggest downfall. I wasn't having any of it, and I suppose that was my biggest mistake. I paid dearly for it later.

AUSTRALIA, MARCH 2006

I finally left Tom on a bright March day. As soon as I heard the screen door slam behind him on his way to work, I picked up the phone to dial Lydia. She picked up on the first ring.

Without preamble, I said, "I am starting to pack."

Lydia's voice was firm.

"Just throw what you can into the plastic garbage bags that I gave you yesterday. Leave the rest of your belongings until you are settled somewhere."

I pulled in a ragged breath.

"Would you be ready to come as soon as I am finished packing then?"

"Of course. Get moving!"

This task was more difficult than I thought. It hurt to leave so many of my possessions. Tom was vindictive enough to destroy them. I stuffed my photos, mementos and immigration papers into the black plastic bags and reminded myself that I would soon have my freedom. Our neighbors were so close that you could spit on them from the side window. They could easily view our open carport from their kitchen window. I hoped that if they saw me place the bags in Lydia's sister's trunk they would assume I was removing junk from the cabin. Lydia had not visited me here, and her sister's car would not be recognized by anyone watching. This might buy me some time. I would ask Tom for my furniture, pots, pans, and linen once I was in my own place.

Each time I heard a car engine draw near the cabin I panicked.

I realized when I was stuffing my few belongings into the garbage bags what little I had left of my past life. Every time I moved from a place or situation, pieces of me were left behind, scattered like ashes strewn from an urn, never to be made into a whole person again.

Time was passing. I was becoming increasingly nervous. I had a feeling that Tom seemed to sense something was up before he left this morning. I stopped tossing the items I was taking with me in the garbage bags and glanced around me. I had enough things. I needed to leave quickly. I needed to leave, now.

I phoned Lydia to let her know I was ready to be picked up.

She said, "Place the bags near the carport door so we can put them in the car trunk quickly without being seen."

"Good thought. I'll do that now. How long will you be? I'm feeling very edgy."

"The sooner you are out of there, the better. My sister and I are ready to go. See you in a few minutes."

Every second's delay there made me feel more in danger of being caught in Tom's web.

It was only minutes after I hung up that they arrived, but it seemed like an eternity. They pulled up to the cabin and slipped the car into the open carport. We managed to stuff all the bags into Lydia's sister's car very quickly, and soon we were ready to leave. We backed out of the garage and drove out slowly, not wanting to bring attention to ourselves. I did not breathe easily until we reached the highway.

Lydia dropped me off at a motel where I would stay until I found permanent accommodation. I cried tears of relief and exhaustion for the rest of the day. I slept for twelve hours, knowing I was safe for the time being.

I stayed in hiding for several weeks. I established a routine, a quiet life—a shower, an hour's walk in the morning, and one again in the afternoon, a thorough cleaning of my little unit, eating, and then falling into an exhausted sleep. With this schedule, I gradually regained some strength and dignity.

AUSTRALIA, MAY 2006

Through my lawyer, I received word that Tom would not release my belongings until I agreed not to ask for any money from the marriage. I did not have the money to replace my furniture, pots, dishes, cutlery, and linen. My small pension from Canada barely paid the rent at the motel. Much as I'd liked to, I couldn't afford to fight this.

I had to agree to Tom's demands. I didn't have money for the long-drawn-out court appearances Tom would have relished and prolonged. Even then, it took him several weeks to consent to the release of my furniture and paintings.

I arranged for movers to pick up my furniture from Tom's. I also informed the police that I was doing this in case there was a confrontation. They said that they were unable to come to my assistance unless I was assaulted.

The cabin was a fair distance away from the police station. It would take a good half hour for the police to arrive should I require their assistance. Lydia and I would be on our own in an extremely perilous situation.

When moving day arrived, Lydia and I marched into combat up the road to Tom's cabin, arm in arm. The air was hot and dry with a tangent, spicy scent from the eucalyptus trees growing tall along the road, like soldiers in attention. The hot wind that blew insistently did little to cool us off. Although our steps were measured, Lydia would not allow us to lose our confrontational will. We were starkly aware that we faced a cunning and dangerous adversary whose actions were often both erratic and cruelly sadistic. His narcissistic nature would not allow others to see that I had left him.

High above me, I noticed a hawk circle endlessly in the cloudless sky, seeking prey below. My skin began to crawl with jittered nerves. A flicker of white caught the peripheral of my eye. I glanced to my left. It was my neighbor Agnes peeping behind the living room curtains.

Lydia noticed her as well.

"Look, there is Agnes at her window. She has a cell phone in her hand."

I stopped in my tracks. I looked over as the curtain withdrew slowly.

"She's on stakeout! She is going to alert Tom that we are arriving! I trusted her. Oh, my God! We're in trouble!"

Lydia gave my arm a small squeeze.

"Never mind that now. Keep walking."

My mouth was parched. We didn't know what to expect when we got to the cabin. This made us very vulnerable. Our nerves were raw. A flutter in the bushes along the side of the road caused us to jump out of our skin.

Lydia let out a startled cry, "O-ooh!"

A small brown rabbit darted across our path, heading off into the weeds, its white tail flashing as it scurried away.

"We are spooked!" said Lydia, clutching the garbage bags tightly in her hands. We were intending to use them to throw the smaller items in while the movers removed the bigger items.

Lydia moved closer to me and placed her hand under my elbow, urging me forward.

"Come along, one foot in front of the other. Keep moving. We can do this."

When we reached the cabin, I noticed that Tom's car was not in the carport. Where was his car? Was this a trap? Would he honor our agreement and release my furniture? My heart plummeted down to my knees.

Lydia read my thoughts.

"Where is he?"

"He either doesn't plan to cooperate, or he doesn't want to face me. Let's hope it is the latter."

Lydia pulled her light sweater around her and inhaled deeply.

"Try the door. Is it locked?"

I cautiously stepped up to the verandah. The only sound was the hawk's piecing cry as he circled above us. I slowly walked over to the front door. I fumbled for my keys in my pocket, hands shaking. Was he hiding in there, ready to attack us? I placed the key in the lock. It turned half an inch and then stopped.

My heart stopped along with it.

"Oh my God, my God! He's changed the locks!"

Lydia shouted and pulled me away quickly.

"Get away from the door. He might be in there. He might have a gun!"

I now fully understood without question that Tom had an agenda, that he would make trouble, that he would be inside hiding, or that he might sneak up behind us and shoot us, or that he might not show up at all. It could very well be that I would be responsible for Lydia's death as well.

I imagined a dozen eyes from the neighboring cabins watching our every move. I suddenly didn't care what the neighbors thought. Who was I trying to protect?

I sat on the verandah steps and motioned to Lydia to sit beside me. I looked up at the sky and sighted the hawk still soaring above us. All was silent except for the wind chimes near us tinkling merrily. The merry sound was obscene under the circumstances. I wanted to smash the chimes to bits to stop the cheery noise.

Lydia and I sat on the steps in silence for some time. Suddenly, the sun's warm globe disappeared behind a bank of dark clouds. A thunderstorm was building up over the salt lake. I was tired and fearful. I began to despair. We had no choice but to wait for whatever was to happen. The movers would soon be arriving. I would have to turn them away and pay for their time for nothing. I could ill afford that. I was sick with grief and disappointment.

Lydia sat steadfastly beside me. We were silent, unable to fathom what was happening. The movers were late. Lydia kept looking at her watch.

"What do you think he is up to?"

"I am not leaving until the movers arrive," I said, with much more determination than I felt.

The dark green clouds were steadily building up. A stiff breeze rustled the silver leaves in the trees.

I felt both relief and trepidation when I heard the soft rumble of the moving truck's slow clamber up the road. What could I say to them? I wasted their time. As if to confirm my premonition of catastrophe, I spotted Tom's sleek silver Mercedes following closely behind the truck. My heart pitched.

Lydia stood up quickly.

"He must have hidden his car in the bushes up the road. He kept surveillance, watching for us. God help us! He's been watching our every move!"

I was rendered speechless. I felt I was watching a movie, that I was a viewer, not a participant in this horrible drama that was unfolding.

The moving truck continued bumping up the road and then finally screeched to a grinding halt on the curb beside the cabin. Tom's car edged past it and glided into the carport. We heard his car's purr, idling.

Lydia said, "He must be sitting there contemplating or trying to make us wonder what he is up to."

Suddenly, I felt myself slipping into survival mode.

I answered, "He probably likes the drama of it all. I can't allow him to intimidate us. I am done with that!"

Lydia eyed me curiously, as my reply was too nonchalant.

"Are you going to be okay?"

"Yes, I can't let him do this to me."

I noticed the terror in Lydia's eyes.

"Maddy, get a grip! We need to be cautious."

We stepped up to the front door again. We both felt relatively safe while the movers looked on. One of the truckers wore a soft plaid shirt and light blue jeans with strategically spaced rips. He appeared very young and harmless, not the protector I would have cast for the role. Nevertheless, he was standing on the pavement looking alert, watching his partner for a sign. His partner was older. He was tense and formidable, watchful, ready for anything. He wore a black leather vest over a white tee shirt. His well-worked arm muscles gleamed in the heat.

After some time, Tom cut the motor. We heard him open the car door then the door click shut softly. The screen door off the garage snapped open then slammed shut. He entered the house through the door from the garage to avoid facing us.

He wasn't going to make this easy. Was he going to honor his side of the bargain? Or was he going to refuse to let us in? It was hard to know.

I took the plunge, stepped up to the door with a sense of purpose, then knocked loudly. Lydia and I waited at the front door for what seemed like infinity. The movers were restless. I was afraid they might decide the situation was too dangerous and leave.

Trust Tom to make a big deal of this, I thought.

There was no movement inside the cabin that I could discern. I understood that I had to make the first move. I rapped sharply on the door again. Soon Tom's footsteps approached the door. He flung open the door with a theatrical flourish. He was wearing his old blue polyester shorts, worn thin at the pockets, with a blue, faded short sleeved shirt tucked in with a brown belt. The buttons strained over his doughy belly. He looked like a derelict.

There was a moment of thick, airless silence between us. A threat of violence hung heavily in the air. Tension began to build its spiraling twist around and inside us. He stepped aside in an exaggerated gesture to let Lydia and I pass. The movers slipped in quickly behind us.

The sight I witnessed in the middle of the living room shocked me. All my belongings were packed in cardboard boxes, tightly sealed. Anything could be in them.

I could see from where I stood that my best towels were still hanging on the towel rack in the bathroom. My beautiful drapes that I brought from Canada were still on the windows. Obviously, he chose what I could take and what he would keep for himself.

The brooding silence continued. We all stood staring at the boxes so neatly and firmly wrapped and sealed. I was at an impasse. I made a quick decision. I would take the boxes as they were and hope that most of my possessions were in there.

We quickly lifted up the boxes and moved them into the truck. Tom was mute, smoking a cigarette, eyeing us without a word in a slow, cold gaze. As I watched him, I understood irrevocably that he would seek terrible revenge. I also recognized that I was in more danger now than when I was living with him. He was smart. He would realize that I would be in hiding and not tell anyone where I was living. He would find me. When he did, I would be vulnerable, alone, and defenseless.

After spending a few weeks in hiding in a nearby motel, I managed to find a small cottage by the sea. For the first few weeks, I felt out of body, drifting, and alone. By the end of each day, I succumbed to a pervading heaviness.

It was about Tom, of course, but it was also about leaving Canada, and my career and essentially about all the choices I had made in my life so far, choices that were either not thought out well enough or just altogether off the mark. I began to mistrust my ability to connect with people that could love me and my attraction to people that could not.

Also, events that occurred over the past two years did not prepare me to cope with being alone again. At first my entire body was wired tight and tremulous. My mind twisted and whirled and twisted again over the past ordeals. Every night I suffered flash-backs of Tom's violence, a video on continual replay.

I woke up every morning feeling lost, along with a severe headache that I couldn't shake off but eventually learned to live with. I had to work very hard every day to erase the profound memories that haunted me like a specter during the night.

The isolation from friends and family made me even more anxious. I was entirely on my own.

I spent my days on the beach, which was beautiful and isolated. Almost always the beach was deserted. Steep granite cliffs kept people from building houses there. I walked up and down slowly, head uplifted to appear like a woman reflecting, letting the day drift, calm, thinking of the future instead of the worries of the present. Every day I walked along the bluff and down the beach finding shells, driftwood shaped like animals, or objects and stones and glass buffed smooth by the sea. When weariness took over, I trudged home again to make tea and lie down on top of my bed. Again the violent scenes from my marriage to Tom rewound like a movie in my head, playing the horrific scenes over and over.

My headaches seized hold of my life, my neck stiff, my body unyielding, on guard for something terrible to happen.

One day after a long walk on the beach, I decided to relax with a glass of wine on my verandah. The sunlight was dazzling and intense. The palms murmured mildly in the wind. As I settled down into the wicker chair, the bells from the cathedral started ringing.

The clarity and pureness of the sound of the bells grabbed me by the throat. My gullet constricted, and tears streamed down my face in salty rivulets. Through a layer of thick blinding tears, I carefully placed my wine glass on the wicker table beside me.

I tried to pull myself together. Okay, what was happening? I couldn't stop bawling and panting and gasping for air. I was strangely disconnected to what was happening around me. The illogical fragment of me, the fragment wholly captured in the wailing, was the emotion I prohibited myself to face for the past two years. I felt a seismic shift sliding me from grief to anger.

In a flash, I reached a startling insight. Had I not held my emotions incarcerated and locked up deep inside me, I could have wailed like this all day, every day, during the years I spent with Tom. This sudden release of emotions and the liberation of fears allowed me to feel, to hear, and to listen again. My face ran with rivulets of tears and mucus. My throat was raw, but I was alive again, ready to face the world. My chest began to expand, and I started to breathe normally. It hit me then. I had been breathing shallowly for years, almost holding my breath.

As time passed, I increasingly began to regain my balance. The panic attacks that previously stopped me in my tracks without warning waned and now seemed less of a threat. Slowly, slowly, I began to untwist and disentangle my raveled guts. My body slowly began to uncoil and relax.

One day, on impulse, I decided to attend the Anglican cathedral across the street. I gradually became involved in the church's activities. Life became a sweet routine. I began to spend time at a volunteer centre and at the church, teaching English to Sudanese immigrants.

After three years of not knowing how my fate would play out, dazed by the horror show my life had become, I finally began to unwind.

I began to feel a giddy bliss, steering my own life again. I believed what I felt. I belonged to no one. I was removed from any roles. I was no one's daughter, no one's mother, no one's wife—I was just myself. My life became meaningful.

I started to volunteer at the Family Court on Mondays and soon established a routine in my life. A pulsating, guiding light of self-awareness kept beaming, like a beacon beckoning me forward.

TOM'S REVENGE

One day after a long day at the courts, I returned home, content with the day's activities. I poured a glass of red wine and took my glass out to my verandah to catch the salty evening breeze from the ocean. The delicate, warm breeze stirred the eucalyptus trees. The soft swish of the leaves was accompanied by the cicadas' orchestra playing their usual evening performance. The kookaburra's rakish laughter pierced loudly in the distance.

The lights of the homes across the water sparkled gold and white, incandescent as stars, while the sun slipped behind the horizon, gold and red between the water and star-filled night. Contentment washed over me like a satin sheet.

I finished my wine and placed the glass on the wicker table. Then I slipped into the hammock and promptly fell into a lulling, soothing, and unfathomable sleep.

Somewhere, deep in the cottage, my cell phone began to ring. I stirred and lifted myself awake quickly from a dream of the cicadas' chorus. I sat up against my arm to grasp what I was hearing. By the time I pulled myself out of the hammock, the ringing had stopped. It must have been Lydia. I would call back in the morning.

I drifted back to the lowest depth of an ocean of sleep, rose up softly to semi-wakefulness and then slipped back into deep sleep.

The unexpected phone call that interrupted my dreamless sleep disturbed me. It forced me to revert back to many months before. Each time I came up to the shallow wakefulness, there was a gut-churning moment when memories returned to haunt me.

Finally dawn arrived. I kicked back the bed covers and struggled up, still half-blinded by sleep. I walked to the bathroom and splashed cold water on my face. I made coffee. I took my mug onto the verandah and sat down on the steps, lifting my face up to the salty air and to the warm sun.

I nervously checked my cell phone, no message. The phone call last night could not have been urgent. As I sipped my coffee and began to relax, I gazed around me. Seagulls caroused in the sky, joyful under the cloudless sky. Across the street, the church bells began to chime. I looked over to see what was occurring there. A black hearse was parked on the curb. I watched as folks dressed in various shades of black drifted up to the church in a loose line. One or two of the parishioners stopped every few feet to talk quietly to one another.

I sat up with a jolt. For a split second, I thought I saw Tom's weasel face in the crowd. I got up from my chair to secure a closer look at the crowd. It was Tom. I quickly returned to my cabin and locked the door. I pulled the living room curtains shut. As I was walking to the bedroom to close the window, my cell phone rang. I left it on the kitchen counter. This time I raced to get it. I caught my toe on the corner of the wicker chair. This delayed my response to the rings. I righted myself and then reached over to pick it up.

I caught it on the third ring.

"Hello?"

The voice was energetic and firm.

"Hi, there!"

It was Joyce, a co-volunteer from the Family Court. I was surprised. I didn't know her well at all. We met at court meetings, but I did not linger afterwards for coffee. Strangers still made me nervous. I didn't trust anyone. I didn't know the relationship they may have with Tom, so I avoided them. Although I was more relaxed, and I was content to a certain degree, I found that conversations of more than a few minutes made me long for the safety of home and solitude.

My instincts still ran high. Joyce was a person I was cautious with.

I tried to appear cheerful.

"Hi there, yourself!"

Without preamble, she replied, "Are you going into court today?"

"Yes, I am. Why?"

Joyce's voice was breathless and excited. "I have a document for you that you might find interesting. I'll leave it on the coffee table in our meeting room."

I became uneasy, cautious.

"Can I ask what this is about?"

Joyce repeated what she had just said.

"You will find it interesting. I left it there yesterday when I was working. Got to run."

This was the day I volunteered. How had Tom orchestrated this to give it to Joyce the day before I worked at the courts? It enforced my belief that he was stalking me. I rushed to get dressed for court, curious about the document. I convinced myself that I was again being paranoid. The document was probably a change of procedures in the Family Court. I shook off the unease impatiently. I looked forward to my days at Family Court. I felt I made a difference to some people, especially to the divorcing couples and their children. It gave me a chance to think of someone else and not dwell on my own problems.

When I entered the courthouse I went through the usual security check and then up to the main office to obtain the keys to the coffee room. Nothing seemed to be amiss. There was no new buzz in the corridors. Everything seemed normal. Joyce had made much ado about nothing, it seemed. I was more certain that it was just a memo regarding new procedures in the courtrooms.

I turned the keys to the coffee room and opened the door. A large manila envelope was on the coffee table with my name on it in bold letters. Tom's handwriting!

It lay poised there like a snake, on the table, ready to strike. I moved over to pick it up and slipped it into my handbag. Then I put my handbag in my locker. I was late setting up the coffee stall. It would have to wait. My guts were turning over. I became light-headed.

The courts were buzzing. All the divided families and the confused children sat restlessly with their grandparents, aunts, or friends while they waited in the corridor as their parents were inside the courts, destroying their marriages.

During a quick break, I went to my locker, took out the envelope and walked to a quiet place in the courtyard. It was written by Tom.

The words sprung out at me, piercing me in the heart.

"What one shall sow, so shall one reap."

Fear gripped me by the teeth. I stumbled blindly to the concrete bench and sat down.

I read on:

"You may or may not want to read this, but that is of no consequence to me as I have to write my side of the story so the truth comes out.

Oh, Maddy is a smart girl but at times can be too smart for her own good, and this has caused some problems throughout her life, here and in Canada when common sense should have prevailed."

The words kicked in my fogged brain and jolted my guts. I doubled over in pain. I blindly placed the "document" on the bench with my outstretched left arm and pulled air into my deflated lungs. I slowly regained my courage and picked up the document to read on:

He continued, "Should you read the entire document that I have written then you will understand what I am talking about. Me being the innocent pawn in a game that Maddy had to play and pursue for her own benefit."

Tom went on, describing in great deal his version of the last fight we had.

"It all happened on Friday the nineteenth of November, 2004, when I arrived home from work at approx. 1:30 p.m. and held Maddy in my arms and gave her a kiss on the forehead.

"Then I looked into those beautiful eyes and said to her, 'What is wrong?'

"She replied, 'Nothing.' We then went out to do some shopping and arrived home about 4:40 p.m., and as I had not had a beer for about near a month and was not working the following day, which was Saturday, I asked her if it would be okay to go and have a beer with the boys just two houses down the road. When I arrived home a little later she seemed tense and very uncomfortable. (I believe she was about to perform her last act on the stage. This was going to be her final curtain call.) Maddy began to bring things up about the past and tell untruths. I then mentioned to Maddy her absent mindedness and her forgetting things. Then she flew into a rage and told me that she was frightened of me. I knew then that Maddy was very unwell."

These were sick words, so untrue! I forced myself to continue:

"She left me a note. Was this all because of her ego, a domineering effect to make her feel good and superior? It shows the character of the person that wrote it. I will have it analyzed and obtain a profile of her writing."

Tom went on to explain his version of the fight before we left to meet Holly and Ted.

"The truth is that we have a sliding door, and at the bottom of the door is a runner for the door to run in. She had a couple glasses of wine too many and tripped over the runner. I tried to grab her to stop her from falling, and she reckoned that I pushed her. I picked her up from the deck, brought her inside and had a look at her back where there were no immediate marks. I also looked at the back of her head and could not see anything there."

I was stunned! How could he say that I fell on my head and back if I tripped forward? This was insane!

It contained further pages and pages of half-truths and downright lies about my whole life before I met him. I felt myself blanch and began to convulse with hot and cold shivers. I was horrified by the strong, deformed bitterness that Tom had harbored these last few years of our marriage. He tarnished my reputation. I fought back a tsunami of nausea. What shocked me most was his ability to twist facts into ugly lies. An invasion of privacy is nothing weighed against reading your life in its entirety, bent and twisted into smut by somebody who has made it their business to obliterate your credibility and good reputation.

My hands shook as I read on. I was tempted to rip the pages into a million pieces, but I continued to read further.

"Maddy dropped out of playing tennis with our neighbors. She stopped playing cards in the afternoons. Did some of these women catch her out with the fabricated stories she told them?"

This was so unfair! I stopped those activities because I was embarrassed at the abuse I received from Tom. I knew I was the topic of many of their conversations. They felt sorry for me, being in that predicament. I couldn't stand their pity.

Tom ranted on: "I haven't seen any photos of Maddy and her children: There seems to be a big gap in Maddy's life. I feel that I should find out why. I should do some research on her."

I was as exposed and vulnerable as a bug under a microscope. Trouble was, the truth would not be seen. The bug on the slide would be so distorted that it would be unrecognizable.

Tom was my husband, a man I once trusted. I had told him about my mother, how terrified I had been of her, and of Erin's pregnancy, and what a destructive force within my family this had been. I told him how much I missed Erin, how lonely I was.

I spoke about Father, too, how I quietly idolized him, how confused I was about him. It was only then that I realized how angry I was that he didn't do more to help the family's distress.

My hands began to shake so violently that it was difficult to read the lines. I pushed on.

"THINGS I BELIEVE MADDY HAS NOT TOLD ANYONE!!!"

I willed myself to go on. It was imperative that I continue. I had to know what Tom was saying about me. He addressed these pages to his sister, but in the deepest core of my being, I knew he had sent this filth to others. He needed to justify why I left him.

"I went through some tapes that Maddy had in her desk. I came across one which was marked 'Harassment.' I put it on my computer to see what it had on it, but it had been cleared. So, it looks like Maddy has been taking notes to record things about me. Who did she give it to? Only thing, it has to be lies. What is the purpose of these notes? I will have to put a stop to this!"

This was an old tape I had in a box of my course material. It was a workplace harassment course.

An upsurge of acidic vomit erupted through my throat and splashed into my mouth. I quickly raced up the hall to the washroom. I barely made it to the stalls before I up-surged. I sat limply on the cold tile, the life drained out of me. Soon I heard the bathroom door open and footsteps on the hard tile. I had to pull myself up and pull myself together.

When I came out of the bathroom stall I saw Pauline, a lawyer I admired. I was mortified. I felt like a lunatic. My eyes were streaming, my nose was streaming, and I was pale as a ghost.

Pauline looked at me with concern.

"Everything all right? Anything I can do? You look like you've seen a ghost."

"No, I'm fine."

She couldn't get away fast enough.

"If you're sure I can't help?" My heart sank. I had lost so much dignity in the last two years. I don't think I could cope with anymore censure or pity. Volunteering here was my chance to regain some self-esteem. Tom had managed to spew his venom here now, too.

In a daze, I went to the sink and splashed cold water on my face and repaired my makeup. I left the washroom and sat for awhile in the empty courtroom. The courtroom soon started to fill up again for the afternoon session. I stood up and walked back to the coffee stall. A woman, who looked in worse shape than me, walked up to my table and asked for a cup of coffee. Her hands were shaking uncontrollably as she poured some cream into her cup. I assumed she was going into the divorce court shortly. I knew too well what she was going through. Between serving coffee to the court's participants, I had a chance to think things through. Tom's lies, deceit and everything he was doing was beyond my comprehension. He must have authored the filth on the pages after I left, twenty pages of outrageous lies. Why did he do this? It must have taken Tom a great deal of time to type this. I imagined him pecking away with two fingers at the computer keys for hours at a time, seething with anger.

My mind swirled around and around this image like a cyclone. Colossal outrage must have fueled him. What did this mean? Why did he turn half-truths into ugly slander? Also, I was frightened by his stalking. What was his purpose? Was he hoping to catch me with another man? He would be crazy to think that. Was he trying to find me in any compromising position that he could blackmail me with? Would he try to scare me off from asking for any money from the marriage? Anything was possible. I couldn't believe that he could be so vindictive—or yes, I could. I had seen him with others. After watching him during the last year, I could believe he would do anything. Tom found a lethal missile then fired it. I realized that I had been expecting something terrible to happen all along. This was truly a shock and awe campaign against me. He couldn't stand that I was the one that left. No one left him. He was beyond reproach.

I went down to the cafeteria to purchase a coffee. I needed to clear my head before I started for home. I sat at a table away from the crowd to try to make some sense of what was happening. Once I began to think clearly, the mist suddenly dispersed.

I think that there is an instant in every liaison where you can catch a glimpse of its whole entity if you are in tuned to it. I finally understood clearly through the marital fog that I had been enmeshed in that Tom had distanced me from my family, my friends, and my coworkers by turning half-truths into lies all along. When I looked back, I realized that it was not only with this document that he did this. I suddenly realized that over the past two years he had systematically and very methodically worked to undermine and completely alienate my friends and family from me. Now he was out to destroy my reputation in its entirety. He tainted all I had confided in him, then twisted it, exaggerated it, and made me look like a monster, an unfit mother, and a loser.

The cafeteria began to thin out. People were leaving quickly. Thunder rolled and rumbled in the distance. Lightning sliced through the dark sky. I promptly gathered my things up and fled the court house.

The predicted storm had arrived in a fury. Palm trees were bent over in half and swaying crazily back and forth in frenzy in the fierce wind. I ran, dashing to my car through the driving rain. Huge splats of ice-cold water fell on my face, shoulders, and down my neck. Water streamed down the pavement, winding its way down, then spun around and around feverishly, down a gurgling drain.

The calm I felt earlier left me. I fumbled with my car keys to unlock the car door, becoming thoroughly soaked during the process.

Once in, I started the engine, but I was too weak to carry on. I let the car idle, sinking down in the seat, my heart thumping wildly in my chest. I placed my head on the steering wheel, exhausted from emotion. I started to weep loudly. I sat up and I hammered my fist on the steering wheel. The resulting pain brought a surprising relief.

Finally, I cried myself out, wet and chilly now, inside and out. Rain still poured in a relentless stream over the car's roof, over the windshield, and then over the hood like a gushing waterfall.

I peered into the rearview mirror before backing out of my parking space. It was fogged up. Squiggly red and white lights shone in abstract through the mist. I was unable to see the oncoming traffic, but I took a chance and backed up in a snail's pace to enter into the moving traffic. Although it was only late afternoon, it was as dark as midnight. My wipers dashed back and forth frantically but were powerless to stem the pouring torrent racing erratically over the windshield.

Traffic slowed to a crawl. I was impatient to get home. I backed up to the curb then with little caution pulled into the stream of cars. Traffic was so agonizingly slow. I passed the car in front recklessly. Suddenly I collided with a sizable puddle and hydroplaned to the right. I spun my car to the left into the spin slowly, just avoiding oncoming traffic. I was sick with relief. A layer of water swished loudly under my wheels, slowing me down with the rest of the cars.

I finally reached home. I pulled into my garage and turned off the motor quickly. I took a cursory look through my rearview window before leaving the car. I was cautious and wary now. I sensed Tom's presence. I needed to get out and close the garage door in case Tom was lurking close and could slip into the garage. I glanced up through the rearview mirror again before I got out of my car. Tom may have slipped in. In that case, I would lock the car door and back up out of the garage.

Tom's car was slowly pulling out from the curb across the street. My raw instinct was right. Tom had been following me. And he wanted me to know.

I warily stepped out of the car and opened the side door to the house off the garage and slipped into my house. I kicked off my wet shoes, pulled off my soaked socks in the hallway, dropped them there, and then I peeled off my sodden clothes as I walked to the bedroom to change into something dry.

I quickly changed out of my wet clothes and put on my jeans and tee shirt. I made directly to the phone to call Lydia. I had to make some sense out of this horrifying nightmare.

Thankfully, Lydia picked up the phone on the first ring. I was so relieved that she was on the other end of the line. She was my anchor in this terrible tempest.

I twisted the cord around and around my wrist as I spoke with her.

"It's not a bad time to call, is it?" I said anxiously.

Lydia sensed my panic.

"What's wrong?"

Hearing her strong voice, I folded.

"Oh God, oh God, everything, oh Lydia, it's so terrible!"

"Hold on. I'll get my chair and bring over my tea."

I was breathless. I didn't realize how tense I was until I heard Lydia on the other end of the line. She listened without interruption, although I heard a gasp or an expletive now and then.

When I talked myself out and paused, Lydia exploded.

"Is he nuts? Who did he send it to? Do you know?"

"I don't know. I don't know how Joyce got it. I haven't phoned her. Really, I am afraid to find out." My throat constricted. I couldn't speak for a moment. I continued. "I realize now that half the time he lies on purpose, and half the time he just lies for no reason."

Lydia paused before answering me, then said, "Sounds pathological to me. You'd better protect yourself and do so quickly!"

She went on to say, "Tom is so egotistical that he doesn't want anyone to think you left him because of anything he has done. Anyone that knows you knows that the contents of the document are lies."

I knew I was out of control, but I couldn't stop myself. I yelled at Lydia, my only ally, the last person I should shout at.

"People believe the worst of anyone. You know that they do!"

"Maddy, listen. You need to hire a new lawyer and a detective, pronto. Legal Aid will take too long. You are in danger. Don't put it off. I mean it. I am going to phone you in the morning to make sure you've done that. I am not letting this go. You cannot ignore this. I won't let you."

FIRST LAWYER

After a feeble good-bye, I hung up then immediately went to search in the yellow pages for the name of a lawyer before I lost my nerve. I was in luck. I found one whose office was nearby. I phoned immediately to arrange for an appointment for the next day.

The next morning I woke in a thick miasma. My brain was fogged down in Tom's insane outburst of lies. I stumbled into the shower half awake. I walked into the kitchen, hair soaked, cold droplets of water dripped onto my shoulders. Coffee, I needed coffee.

As I ambled toward the kitchen counter, I noticed the document that lay on the kitchen table. I felt compelled to pick it up. It pulled me in, like a drug. I had not finished reading the contents. I had to know everything he had said so I could protect myself. I was sick with anxiety and bone tired. Part of me wanted to discard the whole thing and forget it, but I knew that I couldn't afford the luxury.

The page where I had left off started:

"FINAL SUMMARY

This summary will find and depict the misfortunes that show Maddy is not really to blame for the actions she has taken. It will also depict some of the answers to the questions that I have mentioned in the previous notes called, 'Maddy.'"

Is he really going to say I am insane, and that is why I left him? I was Alice in Wonderland, falling down the hole to a scary fantasy land. What will I find there in his imaginative world?

"Maddy and her neighbor were very close. Thinking back now, there were photos of them at a park. Lydia had her arm around

Maddy's shoulder at one point. So, maybe I am right, maybe I am wrong, but they were quite close. Maybe this is why she left me?

Maddy took to reading a great deal of books, all fiction, and whether she was trying to act out what she had been reading or could not come to grips with real life, I don't know."

He went on the say that I had been raped by a man in a park. I had been abused by the inmates I worked with at the penitentiary when I was a case management clerk. I was abused by the officers I worked with at the Department of National Defense. I was abused by my co-workers at BC Centre for Disease Control. He did this all to further his case that I was insane, and that is why I left. Wouldn't Dr. Phil have fun with this?

I put the document down, drank down my coffee in a few gulps, burning my tongue in the process, then slipped my sandals on and walked out the door, letting the screen door slam shut loudly behind me.

The next morning was gray and foggy. It suited my dreary mood. I decided to walk along the ocean to clear my head. I kept looking over my shoulder for Tom. I was paranoid. I kept my eye on the time. It was getting late. I headed for home, changed my clothes, raced to my car and then sped to the appointment with my lawyer.

The law office was housed in a red brick building on Main Street overlooking the ocean. A bold iron-cast lion on each side of the marble steps guarded the front entrance to the ancient historical building. I felt intimidated by the grandeur of the lobby as I entered the front door. I went over to the elevator and looked up the office number of my lawyer. His office was on the top floor. I realized suddenly that I had made a colossal mistake. He might be terribly expensive. I decided to keep my appointment anyway and then make the decision whether to continue with him after I saw him. I would need a formidable protector on my side. The cost of the fee might be worth it in the long run. I had arrived early. When I entered the reception area, I was thankful to see that there was no one waiting before me. No one was at the reception desk, either. I glanced around me. The office was sterile and cold. A black leather sofa was placed in front of a blank white wall.

Magazines were placed precisely in a neat pile on a spotless glass coffee table. I walked over to the reception desk. It was bare with the exception of a black telephone and a notepad. The office seemed deserted.

I called out, "Anyone here?"

A loud, raspy female voice screeched from the inner depths of an office down the hall.

"Don't get your knickers in a knot. I'm coming!"

The woman who entered the reception area was in sharp contrast to the sterile atmosphere of the office. She seemed to be in her mid-fifties, but she appeared to be in somewhat of an identity crisis, kidding herself that she was still in her mid-thirties. She wore designer, over-large Christian Dior animal print glasses. Her glossy makeup was so thick you could peal it off with a spatula. She wore a tight, black dress falling a little short of her ass. Her dirty-blonde hair was frizzy and unruly, somewhat like you might see in a child's stick drawing. She looked like an old neglected Barbie doll that had lain in a girl's dusty toy box forever. She appeared so fragile that you would be afraid to bump into her in case she broke into a hundred pieces.

She snapped her gum, pushed her glasses up to the bridge of her nose then peered at me.

"You got an appointment, doll?"

"I am here to see a Mr. Brown?" I wondered at that moment if I should have done more research on finding a lawyer. *Should I just walk out the door?*

"Have a seat, darling. I'll see if he can see you now."

She left me in a rush, a dozen silver bracelets clashing together like tiny cymbals on her thin wrist. Her stiletto heels clicked down the hall. She pranced down the hall like a small pony to enter the office she had just come from.

I heard her say, "Your appointment is here."

From the office came a male's rough growl in reply, "Shut the door."

After a few minutes, the doll-baby-receptionist reentered

the reception area, looking even more disheveled and seeming more than a little flushed. She pulled at her skirt at the waist to right it and then tugged the hem down impatiently. She then looked up but did not meet my eyes.

"He's ready for you now."

I followed her down a narrow hall lined with black and white architectural drawings of historical buildings of the area. At the end of the hall, she opened the door to a large office, and without preamble hurriedly turned around and sped off.

When I entered the office, I was surprised to see an elegantly dressed man in his early seventies fussily lining up files in exact formation on his desk. His bow tie was tight against his neck, looking as if it were holding up his Adam's apple. His black suit was a perfect fit. His snow-white shirt was immaculate. Expensive gold cuff links twinkled against his starched cuffs. He scrutinized the order of his files on his desk for a moment and then looked up. His eyes inspected me like a specimen in a lab experiment.

His voice was indifferent. He drawled lazily.

"You want a divorce, I understand."

With resolve, I said, "Yes, I do."

He picked up a toothpick off his desk and proceeded to pick at his front teeth.

"The reason?"

"He drinks. He beats me."

His dull eyes said it all. His apathy to my dilemma was stark and open.

"It's difficult to prove abuse. Do you have hospital bills, witnesses? Are things really that bad?"

The sick realization that this man would not be an ally hit me like a ton of bricks. He viewed me as a Canadian, in her mid-fifties, past the bloom of youth. He thought I should accept what Tom dished out. I was past my use-by date and a foreigner as well.

The disappointment felt rock-heavy in my chest. I was stymied, but I knew it was crucial not to stand still to this abuse. Without any conscious thought, I knew that I must move forward to find sanity or freeze in this fear. I walked out of the office without a word, slamming the door behind me. I would have to find another way.

I realized then that I needed to find proof that Tom abused me. I also needed to know why he was receiving those clandestine phone calls. Once again, I pulled out the yellow pages, this time in search of a detective.

THE DETECTIVE

I found and then arranged to meet with a detective the following week. The day of the appointment I entered the detective's office with some misgivings. I was afraid of what I might find, but the office was small, warm, and welcoming. Photos of a sailboat skimming along the ocean's surface adorned one wall. I wondered if the detective owned the boat. The sofa was soft suede, accessorized with bright, colorful pillows. The square mahogany coffee table was strewn with magazines of all types. The scene could be of someone's living room.

The detective came out of his office to greet me as soon as he heard the bell above the door. He was a starkly attractive man, with dark blond, curly hair, a strong square jaw, and eyes the deep indigo of an evening sky. He wore a soft blue plaid shirt and clean, worn Levi's. His smile lit up the room as he came towards me to shake my hand. His warm expression put me immediately at ease.

He looked directly at me.

"Hi, I'm Garry. Have a seat. Tell me why you are here."

He sat down at his desk and pulled a foolscap pad toward him, then reached for a pen from an oversized coffee mug with a red South Leagues Rugby League motif.

He listened to my story intently, interrupting only to clarify a statement here and there. As my story drew to a close, I began to worry. He was looking off in the distance, silent for a few minutes.

I pulled myself up straight in my chair.

"Will you take it on?"

He was still deep in thought. He placed his elbow on his desk and placed his hands on his chin. A small smile appeared on his kind face as he looked at me.

Mary E. Dickson

"I need a little more information before I unleash the hounds."

I left the office in high spirits, coupled with a new resolve. I was going to get my reputation back, guaranteed! As soon as I left, I phoned Lydia to invite her to dinner to celebrate, and then I headed for the market to pick up two steaks, some salad fixings, and a decadent chocolate cake.

I hurriedly shoved the groceries into the back seat of the car then climbed into the driver's seat. I settled into my car and then looked into the rearview mirror to pull out of the market's parking lot. Tom's silver Mercedes was idling across the street. My heart began to thrum. He must have followed me here. He must now know that I hired the detective. I fell into a cold sweat.

I waited impatiently for a chance to enter the traffic while still keeping an eye on Tom's car. My knees began to shake and knock so badly that I could hardly drive. At last I saw an opening in the steady stream of cars and my chance to speed out into the heavy traffic.

I was able to blend into the line of cars flowing down the highway. I glanced back through the rearview mirror. I was relieved to discover I had lost him.

Dinner with Lydia and her family was bittersweet. Had I not had the encounter with Tom after my meeting with the detective I would have had every reason to celebrate. Thinking about Tom's knowledge that I hired Garry gave me a growing sense of dread I could not shake.

134

LYDIA TETHERS ME TO A RESOLVE

It was fall in Australia. Six weeks passed without incident. Tom for some unknown reason left me alone. The weather had turned cool and windy. Wind blew in through the window sills and beneath my door. I put the little heater on. I took solace in the chill. It had been a long time since I had felt the cold. I hunkered down in my little cabin for a few weeks, relishing the solitude. While I sat before the heater with my coffee, I reflected back to the summer before my father died. I could still remember the smell of the swampy grey mud in the lake bottom. I used to squish my toes in it then let the goo dry on my feet while I lay on the pebbly beach at the shore. I loved the smell of the raspberries growing thick on our vines. Most of all, I loved my cousins, who were my cohorts in everything, from playing run sheep run to playing cowboys and Indians in the bushes near our farms. I dived in, and then swam in happy memories now. For now, in this short time, I was not riddled with angst for the present or the future. The memories of the hell I experienced living with Tom were beginning to recede. It was time to think of my future.

One night, after a brisk walk on the promenade, I received an e-mail from Holly saying that she and Ted would lend me the money I needed to come home. I could stay with them as long as I needed to. She wanted me home, safe. I realized then I needed to make a decision. What am I still doing here? I am a transient now, piling up hours, killing time. Tom was still a danger, lying in wait in the background. He could strike at any time.

I had unfinished business here. That was plain, but how could

I clear it up? I did not respond to Holly's e-mail. I placed the request in abeyance. I switched on the small heater, found an easy listening station on the radio then made a cup of tea to enjoy the warmth and the scent of the jasmine tea drifting up to my nose.

I was a dispirited person. I knew that I was not alone in this feeling. It happened to everyone at some point in their lives. I could go home. I could move elsewhere in Australia, somewhere desolate and isolated. Maybe I should move to Lightning Ridge. I would feel at home at a place like that. Not a soul knew me there. I could reinvent myself, be whomever I liked, no history, no ties. Everyone who lived there had a story. I would be no different from anyone else there. I would fit in.

My thoughts were interrupted by a sharp rap on my door. Cold fear raced through me. I ran to the window then slipped the curtain aside. Thank God! It was only Lydia. I was surprised to see her. She usually phoned before she came to see me so I wouldn't be alarmed by the knock on the door. Maybe she was here to tell me more bad news. Or maybe she was just here to catch up because we were, after all, good friends.

Her stride was purposeful as she walked over to my stove.

"Tea?"

The tea in my mug had gone cold. I nodded.

"Yes."

She was silent while the kettle boiled. She had her back to me. I felt suspended, uncertain about what was happening.

I pulled up a shallow breath from my diaphragm.

"What's wrong now?" I felt like a whining child, but I couldn't stop myself from feeling small and defenseless.

Lydia's voice was strong and sure.

"Maddy, you need to learn to fight back!"

Lydia managed with this small statement to bring me to my senses. She had tethered me to a resolve. I was finished with waiting for something to happen. I was finished with the desire to run away from my problems. I contacted my lawyer, and we instigated a defamation suit against Tom.

The upcoming weeks were almost unbearable. I barely slept at night, tossing and turning, getting up for water, then back to bed, tossing some more. Although I had seen neither hide nor hair of Tom recently, I sensed that Tom was still keeping me under surveillance. He was observing my every move, like a cat ready to pounce on a mouse. He must know that our defamation case would be coming up soon, so he wanted to pin something on me. Either that, or he was still so enraged that he wanted to seek further revenge. He may in his crooked thinking want to kill me so his reputation would remain unsullied.

The weeks dragged by slowly. I hadn't heard any news from Garry. I began to doubt my initial impression of him. I began to lose faith in everyone. I began to lose faith in myself again.

The next week, though, just as I had completely given up hope, I received a surprise phone call from Garry.

He said without preamble, "Maddy, did you tell me that Tom was receiving strange phone calls while you were with him?"

His question took me by surprise.

"Yes, but what would that have been about?"

"He was blackmailing his boss. His boss was skimming money from the profits. Tom was aware of this. Keep this between you and me. I will make further inquiries. We will get to the bottom of this. Don't worry."

Garry did not contact me for a few weeks. My nerves were rubbed raw. I was beginning to wonder if he was really on to something, or if it was another false lead. I hadn't had a glance of Tom anywhere. This was just as alarming as seeing him appear out of nowhere. What was he up to?

As the day of the defamation hearing approached, I grew more and more edgy. I was in a constant red alert. My constant thought was that Tom must realize that he couldn't win this battle. My lawyer and my detective Garry had all the proof we needed to win. His friends may have told him that they were approached by a detective about the material he sent out. The closer we came to the court date, the higher level of danger I was in.

The next week, just as I was preparing my dinner, the phone

rang. I walked over to answer it with a feeling of dread. These days, no news was good news.

I picked it up as if it would give me an electric shock.

"Hello?"

"Hi." It was Garry. Thank God! His voice was excited and triumphant.

"Maddy, turn on your TV to channel six. They are announcing a news bulletin. I called the media. I wanted to get as much public humiliation for Tom as possible. This won't tame him, though. Don't be surprised if he still thinks the rest of the whole world is wrong."

"What's this about?" I asked, catching the excitement in Garry's voice.

"Hang up, and put the TV on, or you'll miss it!"

I barely said good-bye. I let the telephone cord dangle as I reached for my remote then punched in channel six. I clicked on the channel. I watched in awe. Tom was being led away in handcuffs by a sheriff. He raged like a speared bull. He swayed his head back and forth like a roped animal and screamed.

"I'll sue the pants off you for false arrest! I am innocent!"

I couldn't help but see the irony in the scene. Tom couldn't bear authority. Also, he was arrogance personified. When people approached to talk to him, he was almost always condescending. Now he was like a trapped animal, gnawing at his chains, growling. This was irony personified. He was so intent on saving his reputation at all costs, and here he was on TV, losing it so publicly.

It was a scene from a two-star movie. It took me a while for reality to sink in. Then I realized that it was all over. Surprisingly, I felt sorry for Tom. This was not the catharsis I imagined I would feel. I was sorry also that our marriage ended on such a sad note. No further threats or whispers could threaten me any longer. I didn't even have to take him to court.

Tom did one important thing for me, though. I started to rethink the course my life could take. Never again would I allow anyone to control me. I realized that there was a seduction of sorts. Tom made me feel safe and protected at first, but slowly and insidiously, his controlling began to become stronger and stronger as I became weaker and weaker. His narcissistic nature made him feel I was an extension of him.

I turned off the TV and took my coffee onto the veranda. I settled into my wicker chair. The sun was slowly sinking in the west, casting a golden glow over the eucalyptus trees. My mind rewound the movie of events I had just witnessed on the TV. It was surreal. Years from now, Tom's amazing downfall and my resulting freedom would define tonight for me, the conclusion of one part of my life, the commencement of another. But for now, I was free to return home to Canada and my family. But that's another story.